CAPTAIN PAUL

by

Alexandre Dumas

British Library Cataloguing-in-Publication Data
A catalogue record for this book is available from the
British Library

Contents

Alexandre Dumas

Alexandre Dumas was born in Villers-Cotterêts, France in 1802. His parents were poor, but their heritage and good reputation – Alexandre's father had been a general in Napoleon's army – provided Alexandre with opportunities for good employment. In 1822, Dumas moved to Paris to work for future king Louis Philippe I in the Palais Royal. It was here that he began to write for magazines and the theatre.

In 1829 and 1830 respectively, Dumas produced the plays Henry III and His Court and Christine, both of which met with critical acclaim and financial success. As a result, he was able to commit himself full-time to writing. Despite the turbulent economic times which followed the Revolution of 1830, Dumas turned out to have something of an entrepreneurial streak, and did well for himself in this decade. He founded a production studio that turned out hundreds of stories under his creative direction, and began to produce serialised novels for newspapers which were widely read by the French public. It was over the next two decades, as a now famous and much loved author of romantic and adventuring sagas, that Dumas produced his best-known works – the D'Artagnan romances, including The Three Musketeers, in 1844, and The Count of Monte Cristo, in 1846.

Dumas made a lot of money from his writing, but he was almost constantly penniless as a result of his extravagant lifestyle and love of women. In 1851 he fled his creditors to Belgium, and then Russia, and then Italy, not returning to Paris until 1864. Dumas died in Puys, France, in 1870, at the age of 68. He is now enshrined in the Panthéon of Paris alongside fellow authors Victor Hugo and Emile Zola. Since his death, his fiction has been translated into almost a hundred languages, and has formed the basis for more than 200 motion pictures.

INTRODUCTION.

The admirers of "The Pilot," one of the most magnificent of Cooper's novels, have evinced a general feeling of regret, in which we ourselves have deeply participated, that the book, once finished, we altogether lose sight of the mysterious being whom we had followed with such intense interest, through the narrows of the Devil's Grip, and the Cloisters of St, Ruth. There is in the physiognomy, in the language, and in the actions of this person, introduced in the first place by the name of John, and afterwards under that of Paul, a melancholy so profound, a grief so bitter, a contempt of life of so intense a nature, that every reader desires to become acquainted with the motives which influenced so brave and generous a heart. For ourselves, we acknowledge that we have more than once been tempted, however indiscreet, to say the least of it, it might have been, to write to Cooper himself, and ask him for information regarding the early career and closing years of this adventurous seaman—information which we have vainly searched for in his narrative. I thought that such a request would be readily forgiven by him to whom it was addressed, for it would have been accompanied by the expression of the most sincere and ardent admiration of his work; but I was restrained by the reflection that the author himself, perhaps, knew no more of that career, of which, he had given us but an episode, than that portion of it which had been illuminated by the sun of American Independence: for, in fact, this brilliant meteor had passed from the clouds which environed his birth to the obscurity of his death in such a manner, that it was quite possible the "poet historian," being far distant from the place where his hero was born, and from the country in which he died, knew no more of him than what he has transmitted to us. The very mystery which surrounded him, may have been the cause of his selecting Paul Jones to play a part in his annals. Urged by these considerations, I resolved upon obtaining, by my own research, those details which I had so often desired to receive from others. I searched through the archives of the Navy; all I found there was a copy of the letters of marque granted to him by Louis XVI. I examined the annals of the Convention; I only found in them the Decree passed at the time of his death. I questioned his contemporaries; they told me that he was buried in the cemetery of Père la Chaise. This was all the information I could gather from my first attempts.

I then consulted our living library—Nodier, the learned—Nodier, the philosopher—Nodier, the poet. After reflecting for a few moments, he mentioned a small book written by Paul Jones himself, containing memoirs of his life, bearing this motto, "Munera sunt Laudi." I started off to hunt for this precious relic; but it was in vain I searched through libraries, rummaged the old book-stalls—all that I could find was an infamous libel, entitled, "Paul Jones, ou Prophétie sur l'Amérique, l'Angleterre, la France, l'Espagne et la Hollande" which I threw from me with disgust, before I had got through the fourth page, marvelling that poisons should be so enduring, and be perfectly preserved, whilst we search in vain for wholesome and nutritious food—I therefore renounced all hope in this quarter.

Some time afterwards, while taking a voyage along our coast, having started from Cherbourg, I visited St. Malo, Quimper, and l'Orient. Upon my arrival at the latter place I recollected having read in a biography of Paul Jones, that this celebrated seaman had been three times in that port. This circumstance had struck me—I had noted down the dates, and had only to open my pocket-book to ascertain them. I examined the naval archives, and in them I actually found entries of the sojourn which the two frigates, the Hanger, of eighteen guns, and the Indienne, of thirty-two, had made in these roads. As to the reasons for their coming there, whether from ignorance or neglect, the secretary who had kept the register had omitted to assign them. I was just leaving the office without further information, when I thought of inquiring of an old clerk who was sitting there, whether there was no traditional recollection in the country as to the captain of these two ships. The old man told me that in 1784, he being then a boy, and employed in the Quarantine Office at Havre, had seen Paul Jones there. He was at that time a commodore in the fleet of the Count de Vaudreuil. The renowned courage of this officer, and his extraordinary exploits, had made such an impression upon him, that upon his, the clerk's, return to Brittany, he spoke of him to his father, who then had charge of the Chateau d'Auray. Upon hearing the name of Paul Jones, the old man started, and made a sign to him to be silent—the young man obeyed, though not without astonishment. He frequently afterwards questioned his father upon the subject, but he always refused to satisfy his curiosity. It was not till after the death of the Marchioness d'Auray, the emigration of her son, the Marquis, and the dispersion of the family at the Revolution, that the old man felt himself permitted to reveal, even to his son, the strange and mysterious history, in which that of the object of my inquiries was so singularly blended. Although nearly, forty years had passed away since his father had related that eventful history, it had made so deep an impression upon him that he repeated it to me, as he assured me, nearly word for word.

I have treasured up this history in the recesses of my memory for nearly seven years: and it would have still remained buried there, with a mass of other recollections, destined never to see the light, had I not about six months ago read "The Pilot" for the second time, and even with much greater interest than before; for, thanks to the researches I had made, the hero was no longer to me an unknown being, appearing only for an instant, his face but partially visible, and with merely the portion of a name; he had now become a friend, almost a brother, to me—for new sympathies had been awakened in my heart besides those which had formerly been inspired by the recital of the expedition to Whitehaven. These led me to reflect that whatever of interest and disappointment I had experienced on reading' Cooper's novel, they must have been entertained alike by others, and that the anxious desire I had felt to know more of the former lover of Alice Dunscombe was not a feeling peculiar to myself, but would be participated by all those, and their number must be great, who have followed this skilful seaman from the moment of his first meeting Lieutenant Barnstaple on the English cliffs, until that in which he quitted the Alert to land on the shores of Holland.

I have, therefore, gathered up my recollections, and have written this history.

CHAPTER I—A STRANGE SAIL

Hoarse o'er her side the rustling cable rings-
The sails are furled—and anchoring, round she swings;
And gathering loiterers on the land discern
Her boat descending from the latticed stern.
'Tis mann'd—the oars keep concert to the strand,
Till grates her keel upon the shallow sand.—   *Byron.*

Toward the close of a fine evening in the month of October, 1779, the most inquisitive among the inhabitants of the small town of Fort Louis, had assembled on the point of land immediately opposite to that on which stands the city of Lorient. The object which attracted their attention, and which was the subject of their inquiries, was a noble beautiful frigate, carrying 32 guns, which had been anchored for about a week, not in the port, but in a small cove in the roadstead, and which had been perceived for the first time early one morning, like an ocean flower which had suddenly blossomed during the night. From the elegant and coquettish appearance of this frigate, it was imagined that this was the first time of her putting to sea; she bore the French flag, for the three golden fleur-de-lis were seen glittering in the last rays of the setting sun.

That which, above all, appeared to excite the curiosity of the admirers of this spectacle, so frequent, and notwithstanding, always so interesting in a seaport, was the uncertainty as to the country in which this vessel had been built; for, having all her sails clewed up and snugly stowed around her yards, showed in the setting sun the graceful outline of her hull, and a minute elegance as to her running rigging. Some thought they could discern in her the bold and taunt masts used by the Americans, but the perfection exemplified in the finish which distinguished the rest of her construction, was in perfect contrast with the barbarous rudeness of those rebellious children of England. Others, deceived by the flag she had hoisted, were endeavouring to divine in what port of France she had been launched, but their national pride soon gave way to the conviction that she was not built in France, for they sought in vain for those heavy galleries, ornamented with sculpture, which is the compulsory decoration of the stern of every daughter of the ocean, or of the Mediterranean, born on the stocks of Brest or of Toulon; others, again, knowing that the flags were frequently used as a mask to hide the real face, maintained that the lion and the towers of Spain would have more properly been placed upon the ensign waving from her peak, than the three fleur-de-lis of France: but the latter were asked whether the straight and elegant sides and quarters of the frigate all resembled the bulging build of Spanish galleons. In short, there were some among them who would have sworn that this beautiful fairy of the waters had been brought to life among the frogs of Holland, had not the dangerous boldness of her masts and rigging fully contradicted the suggestion that she could have been built by those old but prudent sweepers of the seas. But, as we have said, for eight whole days, and ever since the first appearance of this splendid vision upon the coast of Brittany, she had been the constant theme of wonder and of conversation, for nothing had happened to give them any positive information, as not an individual from the crew had landed from the ship, under any pretext whatever. They might, indeed, have doubted whether she had a crew or not, had not they now and then seen the head of a sentinel, or of the officer of the watch, peering above the bulwarks. It appeared, however, that this vessel, although she had not communicated with the shore, could not have any hostile intention; her arrival had not seemed to give the least uneasiness to the public authorities of Lorient, for she had run under the guns of a small fort, which the recent declaration of war between England and France had caused to be put in order, and which displayed a battery of long guns of heavy calibre.

Among this crowd of idlers, however, there was a young man, who was remarked for the anxious eagerness of his inquiries:—without any one being able to devise the cause, it was easily perceived that he felt some direct interest in this mysterious vessel. His brilliant uniform was that of the mousquetaires, and as these royal guards rarely left the capital, he had, at first, directed a portion of the public curiosity to himself, but it was soon discovered that this person, whom they thought a stranger, was the young Count d'Auray, the last scion of one of the most ancient families of Brittany. The castle inhabited by his family rose above the shores of the Golf of Morbihan, at six or seven leagues, distance from Fort

Louis. The family consisted of the Marquis d'Auray, a poor insane old man, who for twenty years had never been seen beyond the boundaries of his estates; of the Marchioness d'Auray, whose rigid morality, and whose ancient nobility, could alone excuse her haughty and aristocratic bearing; of the young Marquerite, a sweet girl of seventeen or eighteen years of age, delicate and pale as the flower whose name she bore; and of Count Emanuel, whom we have mentioned above, and around whom the crowd had gathered, carried away, as it always is, by a sounding title, a brilliant uniform, and noble and lordly manners.

However eager might have been the desire of those he addressed to satisfy his curiosity, they could only answer his questions in a vague and undecided manner; all they knew of the frigate being mere conjecture. The count was about retiring from the jetty, when he perceived a six-oared boat approaching it. At a moment when curiosity had been so much excited, this incident could not fail to attract all eyes. In the stern of the boat sat a young man, who appeared to be from twenty to twenty-two years of age, and who was dressed in the uniform of a lieutenant of the royal navy— he was sitting, or rather lying, upon a bearskin, one hand reclining carelessly on the tiller of the small boat, while the coxswain, who, thanks to the caprice of his officer, had nothing to do, was sitting in the bow. From the moment that it first made its appearance, every eye was directed towards it, as if it contained the means of solving the mystery which had so much puzzled them. The boat, urged on by the last efforts of its oarsmen, took the ground at eight or ten feet distance from the beach, there being too little water in that place to allow it to come nearer. Two of the sailors jumped into the sea up to their knees. The young lieutenant then rose up in a careless way, walked to the bow of the boat, and allowed the two sailors to carry him in their arms to the beach, so that not a drop of salt water should soil his elegant uniform. He then ordered his men to double the point of land which advanced about three hundred feet into the sea, and to go and wait for him on the opposite side of the battery. As for himself, he stopped a moment on the beach to arrange his dress, which had been a little disordered by the rough mode of transport he had been compelled to adopt, and then he advanced, humming a French air, towards the gate of a small fort, which he passed, after having slightly returned the military salute of the sentinel on duty.

Although nothing could, in a seaport, be more natural than that a naval officer should cross the roads and walk into a fort, the minds of the lookers-on had been so much occupied with the foreign vessel, that there was hardly one among the crowd who did not imagine that this visit to the commandant of the fort had some relation to her, so that when the young officer issued from it, he found himself surrounded so closely by the crowd, that for a moment he appeared half inclined to use the rattan which he carried in his hand, to make way through it. However after having flourished it with impertinent affectation above the heads of those who were nearest him, he appeared all at once to change his mind, and perceiving Count Emanuel, whose distinguished appearance, and elegant uniform, contrasted strikingly with the vulgar air and habiliments of the persons who surrounded him, he made a few steps towards him at the same moment that the count had advanced to meet him. The two officers merely exchanged a rapid glance, but that look at once assured both that they were persons of rank and station. They immediately saluted each other with that easy grace and affable politeness which characterized the young nobility of that period.

"By Heaven!" exclaimed the young midshipman; "my dear countryman, for I suppose that like myself you are a Frenchman, although I meet you in a seemingly hyperborean land, and in regions which, if not absolutely savage, appear sufficiently barbarous—will you have the goodness to tell me what there is so extraordinary about me, that I seem to cause quite a revolution in the country? Or is the appearance of an officer of the navy an event so rare and so extraordinary at Lorient, that his mere presence excites, in so singular a degree, the curiosity of the natives of Lower Brittany? By solving this mystery, you will render me a service which I shall be happy to reciprocate, should any opportunity present itself in which I can be useful to you."

"This will be so much the more easy," replied Count Emanuel, "as this curiosity is not founded in any feeling which you would consider offensive to your uniform or hostile to your person—and the proof of this is, my dear comrade—for I see by your epaulettes that we are of equal rank in the service of his majesty—that I participate with these honest Britons in the curiosity which they evince, although, perhaps, my motives are more weighty than theirs, in endeavouring to obtain a solution of the problem which has occupied us."

"If I can be of any assistance to you, in the inquiries which you have undertaken, I place all the algebra I possess at your disposal. Only the position we are in is not a comfortable one to carry out mathematical demonstrations. Will it please you to remove to a small distance from these honest people, whose presence would only tend to confuse our calculations."

"Certainly," replied the mousquetaire, "and the more readily, as, if I do not deceive myself, by walking this way I shall lead you nearer to your boat and your sailors."

"Oh! that is not of the slightest consequence; should this path not be convenient to you we can take another. I have plenty of time; and my men are less eager to, return on board than I am. Therefore, we will about ship, if such is your good pleasure."

"Not at all; on the contrary, let us go on, the nearer we are to the beach the better we can discuss the matter in question. Let us, therefore, walk upon this strip of land as far as we can."

The young seamen, without replying a word, conti-nued to walk on, like a man to whom the direction he was to take was perfectly indifferent, and these two young men, who had thus met for the first time, walked arm in arm, as though they had been friends from infancy, towards the end of the promontory. When they had reached the extreme point, Count Emanuel paused, and pointed towards the frigate, saying, "Do you know what ship that is?"

The young seaman threw a rapid and scrutinizing glance upon the mousquetaire, and then looked towards the ship: "Yes," replied he, negligently, "it is a pretty frigate carrying two and thirty guns, with her sails bent and her starboard anchor atrip, ready to sail at the first signal given."

"Excuse me," replied Emanuel, smiling; "that is not what I ask of you. It signifies little to me how many guns she carries, or by what anchor she is holding—is not that your technical mode of speaking?"

The lieutenant smiled: in turn. "But," continued Emanuel, "what I wish to know is, to what nation she actually belongs, the port, that she is bound to, and the name of her captain."

"As to the nation she belongs to," replied the lieutenant,

"She has taken care to give us that information herself, or she is, an outrageous liar; Do you not see her flag flying from her peak? It is the flag without a stain, rather worn out from being too much used that's all. As to the place she is bound to, it is as the commandant of the fort told you, when, you asked him,—Mexico." Emanuel looked with astonishment at the young lieutenant. "And finally, as to her captain, that is a much more difficult matter.. There are some people who would swear he is a young man about my own age or yours, for; I, believe we left the cradle pretty closely the one after, the other, although the professions we follow may place a long interval between our graves. There are others who pretend he is of the same age with my uncle the Count d'Estaing, who as you doubtless know, has just been made an admiral, and who is at: this moment affording every assistance to the rebels of America, as some people, even in France, still call them. But, in short, as to his name, that is quite another thing; it is said he does not know it himself; and until some fortunate occurrence shall apprise him of it, he calls himself Paul."

"Paul?"

"Yes, Captain Paul."

"Paul, what?"

"Paul, of the Providence, of the Banger, of the Alliance, according to the name of the ship he commands. Are there not also in France some of our young nobles, who, finding their family name too short, lengthen it out by the name of an estate, and surmount the whole with a knight's casque, or a baron's coronet: so that their seals or their carriages bear the evidence of belonging to some ancient family, quite delightful to reflect upon? Well! so it is with him. At this moment he calls himself, I believe, Paul, of the Indienne, and he is proud of the appellation; if I may judge front my naval sympathies, I do not think he would exchange his frigate for the finest estate to be found between the Port of Brest and the mouth of the Rhone."

"But, tell me," rejoined Emanuel, after reflecting for a moment on the singular mixture of simplicity and sarcasm which pervaded the answers of his companion; "what is the character of this man?"

"His   character—but,   my   dear   baron—count—

marquis"—

"Count," replied Emanuel, bowing.

"Well, my dear count, then, I was about to say that you pursued me from one abstraction to another, and that when I placed at you disposal all my knowledge in algebra, I did not intend that we should enter into a research of the unknown. His character! good heaven, my dear count, who can speak knowingly of the character of a man, unless it be himself— and even then—but hold—I, myself, as you now see me, have ploughed for twenty years, at one time with the keel of a brig, at another with that of a frigate, this vast expanse, which now extends itself before us. My eyes, for so I may express myself, discerned the ocean almost at the same moment that they saw the sky above it; since my tongue was able to join two words together, or my comprehension could combine two ideas, I have interrogated and studied the caprices of the ocean, and yet I do not, even to this time, know its character—and there are only four principal winds and thirty-two breezes which agitate it—that's all. How, then, can you expect that I should judge of man, torn as he is by his thousand passions."

"Nor did I ask you, my dear—duke—marquis—count?"—

"Lieutenant," replied the young sailor, bowing, as Emanuel had done before.

"I was about to say, then, my dear lieutenant, I do not ask a physiological lecture on the passions of Captain Paul. I only wish to inform myself upon two points. Firstly, whether you consider him a man of honor?"

"We must first of all understand each other as to the

meaning of words, my dear count—what is your precise definition of the word honor?"

"Permit me to remark, my dear lieutenant, that this question is a most singular one. Honor! Why, honor—is—honor."

"That's it precisely—a word without a definition, like the word God! God—is God! and every one creates a God after his own fashion. The Egyptians adored him under the form of a scorpion—the Israelites, under that of a golden calf. So it is with honor. There is the honor of Camillus, and that of Coriolanus—that of the Cid, and that of Count Julian. Define your question better if you wish me to reply to it."

"I ask, then, whether his word may be relied upon?"

"I do not believe he ever failed in that regard. His enemies—and no one can arrive to his station without having them—even his enemies, I say, have never doubted that he would keep, even unto death, an oath which he had sworn to. This point is, therefore, believe me, fully settled. In this respect, he is a man of honor. Let us pass, therefore, to your second question, for if I do not deceive myself, you wish to know something farther."

"Yes, I wish to know whether he would faithfully obey an order given by his Majesty?"

"What Majesty?"

"Really, my dear lieutenant, you affect a difficulty of comprehension which would better suit the gown of a sophist, than a naval uniform."

"Why so? You accuse me of cavilling, because, before

replying, I wish to know precisely what I have to answer. We have, at this? present time, eight or ten majesties, seated securely or otherwise, upon the different thrones of Europe. We have his Catholic Majesty—a feeble majesty, who allows the inheritance, left him by Charles, the Fifth, to be torn from him piece by piece;—we have his Britannic Majesty—a headstrong majesty, who clings to his America, as Cyingetus to the Persian ship, and whose hands we shall cut off, if he does not loose his hold;—we have his Christian Majesty, whom I venerate and honor"—

"Well—it is of him I wish to speak," said Emanuel,

"Do you believe that Captain Paul would feel disposed to obey an order which I should deliver from him?"

"Captain Paul," replied the lieutenant, "would, as every captain ought to do, obey every order emanating from a power which has the right of commanding him—unless indeed he be an accursed pirate, or some damned privateersman, some buccaneer, who owes no allegiance, and which I should doubt from the appearance of the frigate he commands, and from the way she is fitted. He must have then in some drawer of his cabin, a commission signed by some power or other. Well! should this commission bear the name of Louis, and be sealed with the fleur-de-lis of France, there can be no doubt that he would obey any order sealed, and signed by the same name."

"This is all then that I wish to be informed of," replied the young mousquetaire, who began to grow impatient at the strange and evasive answers given by his companion. "I will only ask you one more question." "I am ready to obey your wishes in that, as I have in the rest, count," returned the lieutenant.

"Do you know any way of getting on board of that ship?"

"There is one," replied the lieutenant, pointing towards his own boat, which lay rocked, by the waves, in a small creek close to them.

"That boat! why, is it yours?"

"Well! I will take you on board."

"You know this Captain Paul, then?"

"I? not in the least! But as nephew of an admiral, I am naturally acquainted with every officer of a ship, from a boatswain, who pipes the hands aloft, to the rear admiral, who commands a squadron. Besides which, we sailors have secret signs among us, a certain masonic language, by which we know one another as brothers in whatever part of the ocean we may meet. You may, therefore, accept my proposal with the same frankness in which I offer it. I, my rowers, and my boat, are at your disposal."

"Do me this service, then," said Emanuel, "and"—

"You will forgive me the annoyance I have caused by my tergiversations, will you not?" said the lieutenant. "You cannot be surprised at it," continued he smiling, "my dear count, the solicitude of a seaman's life has given to us children of the sea, the habit of soliloquising. During a calm, we invoke the winds! During the tempest, we invoke the calm; and during the night we address ourselves to God."

Emanuel again looked doubtingly at his companion, who

met his gaze with that apparent good tempered simplicity, which had appeared to spread over his features every time he had become the object of investigation, to the mousquetaire. The latter was surprised at this mixture of contempt for human things, and of poetic feeling toward the works of God. But finding that this singular man was disposed to render him, although in a strange manner, the service he had asked of him, he accepted his proffered assistance. Five minutes afterwards, the two young men were advancing towards the unknown vessel with as much rapidity as the vigor of six stout rowers could give to the light bark in which they were seated. Their oars rose and fell with so regular a movement, that it appeared rather impelled by some powerful machine, than by the combination of human strength.

CHAPTER II.—THE FRIGATE.

And oh! the little warlike world within!
The well-reeved guns, the netted canopy;
The hoarse command, the busy humming din-
When, at a word, the tops are mann'd on high,
Hark to the boatswain's call, the cheering cry;
While through the seaman's hands the tackle glides:
Or schoolboy midshipman that, standing by,
Strains his shrill pipe, as good or ill betides,
And well the docile crew that skilful urchin guides.—

Byron.

As they advanced, the graceful form of the ship became
more and more clearly defined, and although the vocation
of the count did not lead him to admire beauty under such
a form, yet he could not avoid being struck by the graceful
model of her construction, the loftiness and strength of her
masts, and the elegance of her rigging, which appeared, as
it stood out against the richly tinted sky, reddened by the
setting sun, to be composed of flexible and silky fibres,
spun by some gigantic spider. There was not, however, any
appearance of movement on board the ship, which seemed,
either from inattention or contempt, to care but little for
the visit she was about to receive. The young mousquetaire
thought, however, at one moment, that he perceived the end
of a telescope peeping out of one of the port-holes, near the
muzzle of a gun, and which was pointed towards the boat;

but the ship being gently moved round by the quiet heaving of the waves, presented her prow toward them, his attention was attracted by the figure-head which generally bears some allusion to the name of the vessel that it decorates: it was a representation of one of the daughters of America, discovered by Columbus, and conquered by Cortez, with a head-dress of many colored feathers, her bosom naked, and ornamented with a coral necklace. As to the remainder of the figure, it was a curious combination, half syren, half serpent, attached to the fore part of the ship in a graceful though fantastic form. The nearer the boat approached the ship, the more did the attention of the count appear attracted by this figure. It was, in fact, a sculpture, not only singular as to form, but very remarkable from the finish of its execution; and it was easy to perceive, that it was not the work of vulgar hands, but had been carved by a superior artist. The lieutenant remarked, with the satisfaction of a seaman, the increasing admiration which appeared in the countenance of the soldier; and at last perceiving that his attention was concentrated in the figure-head we have described, he seemed to wait with impatience that the latter should express his opinion upon it; but finding that he did not give any, although they were near enough not to lose any of its beauties, he took upon himself to be the first to speak, and to question his young companion.

"Well, count," said he, concealing the interest which he took in his reply under an apparent gaiety, "what do you think of this master-piece?"

"I think," replied Emanuel, "that comparing it with

27

works of the same description, which I have seen, it merits the appellation which you have given it."

"Yes," said the lieutenant, carelessly, "it is the last work of William Coustou, who died before he had completed it: it was finished by one of his pupils, named Duprè, a man of genius, who is starving, and who is obliged to carve wood for want of marble, and to cut figure-heads of ships, when he ought to be employed in sculpturing statues. See," said he, giving an impulsion to the rudder which laid then across her bows, "it is a real necklace of coral that she wears, and they are real pearls that are hanging from her ears. As to her eyes, each pupil is a diamond worth a hundred guineas. The captain who takes this frigate, will, besides the honor of capturing her, have a splendid wedding present to offer to his bride."

"What an odd caprice," exclaimed Emanuel, carried away by the singularity of the object he was gazing at, "to ornament a ship in the same way that one would an animated, being, and to risk considerable sums to the chances of a battle, or the dangers of a storm."

"Why should this astonish you?" said the lieutenant with an accent of indescribable melancholy; "we seamen have no other family than our sailors, no other country but the ocean, no gorgeous pageants but the tempest, no amusements but the battle. We must attach ourselves to something, having no real mistresses, for who would love us sea-gulls, who are always on the wing? We must therefore shape to ourselves an imaginary love. The one becomes enamoured of some verdant and shady island, and every time he perceives one in the distance, rising from the ocean like a flower garden, his heart becomes as joyous as that of a bird, when returning to its nest. Another selects some favorite star from out the firmament, and during the long and lovely nights on the Atlantic, every time he passes the equator, it appears to him that it approaches nearer to him, and salutes him with a more vivid light. There are others, and they are the greater number, who attach themselves to their frigate as to a well beloved daughter, who groan whenever the tempest tears away any part of her, at every wound given by the shot that strikes her, and when she is at length sunk by the tempest or the combat, prefer to perish with her, rather than to save themselves without her, giving to landsmen a holy example of fidelity. Captain Paul is one of the latter class, that's all, and he has given to his frigate the wedding present which he had intended for his bride. Ah? I see they are waking up."

"Boat ahoy?" cried some one from on board the frigate, "what boat's that?"

"We want to come on board," replied Emanuel; "throw us a rope that we may catch hold of."

"Go round to the starboard side, and you will find the gangway ladder."

The sailors pulled round, and in a few seconds the two young men were going up the ship's side. The officer of the watch came forward with an eagerness which appeared in Emanuel's mind to promise well.

"Sir," said the lieutenant to a young man who was dressed

in the same uniform as himself, and appeared to be of the same rank, "this is my friend, the Count —— By the by, I forgot to ask your name?"

"Count Emanuel d'Auray."

"I was saying then, that this is my friend, the Count Emanuel d'Auray, who anxiously desires to speak to Captain Paul. Is he on board?"

"He has just this moment arrived," replied the officer.

"In that case I will go below and prepare him to receive you, my dear count. In the meantime, this is Mr. Walter, who will have the pleasure of showing you through the ship. It is an interesting sight for a land officer, and the more so, as I doubt whether you would find many ships kept in such order as this is. The people are at supper just now, I believe?"

"Yes, sir."

"In that case it will be the more curious sight."

"But," observed the officer, hesitating a little, "it is my watch on deck."

"Bah! you can easily find one of your brother officers who will relieve you for a short time. I will endeavour to manage so that the captain shall not make you kick your heels too long in the ante-room. Adieu, till I meet you again, count: I shall recommend you in such a way as will insure a good reception for you." With these words, the young lieutenant disappeared down the companion ladder, while the one who remained with Emanuel to show him over the ship, took him into the 'tween decks.

As the lieutenant had presumed, the crew of the frigate

were at their supper. It was the first time that the young count had been present at such a repast; and however much he desired to speak immediately to the captain, he felt so curious to observe what was going on, that he examined everything with eager attention.

Between every two guns, a table and benches were prepared, not standing on their feet, but slung by ropes from above. Four men were seated upon each of the benches, taking their portion of pieces of beef, which seemed to resist the action of their knives, but which had to do with hearty fellows who did not appear at all disposed to be daunted by its toughness. At every table there were two cans of wine, that is to say, about a pint for each man. As to the bread, it did not appear to be distributed by rations, but they could take as much as they wanted. The most profound silence reigned throughout the crew, which, was composed of of more than from one hundred and eighty to two hundred men.

Although none of those seated at the table, opened their mouths for any other purpose than to eat, Emanuel perceived, with some surprise, that they were composed of many different nations, which was easily discernible from the contour of their countenances. His cicerone remarked his astonishment, and replying to his thought before he had given utterance to it, said, with an American accent, which Emanuel had already observed, and which proved that he who spoke to him was born on the other side of the Atlantic: "Yes, yes, we have a tolerably pretty sample of every nation in the world, and if all at once a good deluge should carry off the children of Noah, as it formerly did those of Adam, our ark could furnish people who speak every language. Do you observe those three fellows who are exchanging a piece of roast beef for a clove of garlick, they are lads from Galicia, whom we picked up at Cape Ortegal, and who would not go into action without having said a prayer to St Jago, of Corapostello, but who, when once their prayer is over, would rather allow themselves to be cut in pieces, like martyrs, than retreat a single step. Those two who are polishing their table at the expense of their jacket-sleeves, are honest Dutchmen, who still complain: of the injury done to their commerce by the discovery of the Cape of Good Hope. You see them—at first sight they look like very beer-pots. Well, those brave fellows, the moment they hear the drum beat to quarters, become as active as monkeys; Go near them, and they will talk to you about their ancestors; they will tell you they descend from those famous sweepers of the sea, who when going into action, hoisted a broom instead of a flag; but they will take good care not to inform you that one fine morning the English took their broom, and made rods of it to whip them with. That whole table, where they are chattering together at such a rate, but in an under tone, is occupied by Frenchmen, who would talk louder if they dared. The seat of honor is occupied by a chief, elected by themselves; he is a Parisian by birth, a cosmopolite from taste, a great master at the small sword, singlestick, and a dancing-master to boot. Always gay and contented, he sings when he is on duty, sings when he is fighting, and will die singing, unless a hemp cravat should stop his voice, which may very likely happen to him should he have the misfortune to fall into the hands of John Bull. Turn your eyes to the other side now, and observe that row of square and idle heads. These are strange faces to you, are they not? but which every American born between Hudson's Bay and the Gulf of Mexico, would recognize at once for bears born on: the borders of Lake Erie, or seals from Nova Scotia.. There are three, or four of them who are one eyed— this arises from, their peculiar mode of fighting; they twist their fingers in the hair of their antagonist, and gouge out his eye with their thumbs. There are some of them who are very expert at this exercise, and who never miss their mark. So that when they are boarding a ship, they almost invariable throw away their boarding, pikes, or their cutlass, and seizing the first Englishman they can catch hold of, they uneye him with a dexterity and quickness quite delightful to behold. You will now comprehend that I did not deceive you in what I said, and that our collection is complete."

"But," asked Emanuel, who had listened to this long enumeration with a certain degree of interest, "how does your captain manage to make himself understood by men brought together from such distant nations?"

"First of all our captain understands all languages—and although in battle and during stormy weather he speaks his mother tongue, he; gives such an accent to it that every one understands him and obeys: him. But see, the larboard cabin door is opening, and I doubt not he is ready to-receive you."

And instantly a boy dressed in a midshipman's uniform

came up to the two officers, and asked Emanuel if he did not call himself the Count d'Auray; and on his receiving an affirmative reply, he requested him to follow him; and the officer who had so conscientiously sustained the part of a cicerone, immediately went on deck to resume his duties there. As to Emanuel, he advanced towards the cabin with a mixed feeling of anxiety and curiosity, He was at last about to be ushered in the presence of Captain Paul.

He was a man who appeared to be between fifty and fifty-five years of age, and to whom the habit of walking between decks had given him a stoop rather than age. He wore the uniform of the French navy, accord-ing to its strictest regulations. It was a blue coat with scarlet facings, a red waistcoat, and breeches of the same color, grey stockings, with frilled shirt and' ruffles. His hair, rolled up in large curls, and powdered quite white, was tied into a queue by a ribbon, the ends of which floated upon his shoulders. His cocked hat and his sword were lying upon a table beside him. At the moment Emanuel entered the door, he was sitting upon the carriage of a gun, but when he perceived him, he rose up to receive him.

The young count felt intimidated by the aspect of this man: there was in his eye a searching look which appeared to peer into the very soul of the person whom he gazed upon. Perhaps, also, this impression was the more powerful, that he presented himself before him with a conscience that reproached him with the act he was endeavouring to accomplish, and of which he was about to render the captain, if not an accomplice, at all events the executioner. These two men, as though they felt a secret repulsion, the one towards the other, saluted each other with politeness, but with cold reserve.

"It is the Count d'Auray that I have the honor of addressing," said the old officer.

"And I Captain Paul, I believe," replied the young mousquetaire; they both bowed a second time.

"May I know to what fortunate chance I owe the honor," rejoined the captain, "of the visit which is now paid to me by the heir of one of the oldest and greatest families in Brittany?"

Emanuel bowed again by way of thanks for this compliment, and then, after hesitating for a moment as if he found it difficult to open the conversation, he observed: "I am told, Captain Paul, that you are bound to the Gulf of Mexico?"

"And you have not been deceived, sir; I purpose sailing for New Orleans, calling on my way at Cayenne, and at the Havannah."

"This falls out very fortunately, captain, and you will not have to alter your course, in case you should be willing to undertake the execution of the order of which I am the bearer."

"You have an order to communicate to me, sir, and from whom?"

"From the Minister of Marine."

"An order addressed to me personally?" reiterated the captain, doubtingly.

"Not personally to you, sir; but to any captain of the royal navy, who may be about to sail for South America."

"Of what nature is it, count?"

"A state prisoner to be transported to Cayenne."

"And you have the order with you?"

"Here it is," replied Emanuel, taking it from his pocket, and presenting it to the captain.

He took the paper, and going near the cabin window, that he might avail himself of the last gleam of daylight, he read aloud:

"The Ministers of Marine and of the Colonies, orders any captain or lieutenant, commanding a government vessel, who may be about to sail for South America, or for the Gulf of Mexico, to take on board his ship and to land at Cayenne, the person named Lusignan, condemned to transportation for life. During the passage the convict shall take his meals in his own cabin, and shall not be allowed to have any communication with the ship's company."

"Is the order in due form?" asked Emanuel.

"Perfectly, sir," replied the captain. "And are you disposed to execute it?"

"Am I not under the orders of the Minister of Marine?"

"The prisoner may then be sent to you?"

"Whenever you will; but it had better be this evening, or as soon as possible, as I do not expect to be long in these roads."

"I will take care that due diligence shall be used."

"Is this all that you have to say to me?"

"Nothing further, excepting to add my thanks."

"Do not add anything, sir. The minister orders, and I obey, that's all. It is a duty which I fulfil, and not a service that I am rendering."

Upon these words, the captain and the count bowed to each other and separated, more coldly even than they had met.

When he reached the deck, Emanuel asked the officer of the watch for his friend who had accompanied him on board, but was informed he had been detained by Captain Paul to sup with him, and that being anxious to oblige the count, he had placed his boat as his disposal.

She was waiting alongside the ship, and the sailors were in readiness to accompany him. Emanuel had scarcely got into her when they rowed him away with a rapidity equal to that with which they had conducted him on board. But this time she proceeded in sorrowful silence, for the young lieutenant was no longer there to animate the count with his practical philosophy.

That same night the prisoner was conducted on board the Indienne, and the next morning at day-break the inquisitive inhabitants of the coast no longer discerned the frigate which had given rise to so many conjectures, and whose unexpected arrival, her remaining there without any apparent object, and her spontaneous departure, remained an inexplicable mystery to the inhabitants of Fort Louis.

CHAPTER III.—THE SEA FIGHT.

The gallant vessels side by side did lie,
Yard-arm and yard-arm, and the murd'rous guns
Belch'd forth their flame and shot, 'till the white decks
Ran like a sea with blood. Uncertain still
The victory stood, 'till Perry, waving
His bright sword o'er his head, cried, "Follow me!"
A hundred shouts responded to this call,
Then with one spring he bounded on the deck
Of his determined foe.

—Oxd Play.

As the motives which had induced Captain Paul to visit the coast of Brittany had no relation with our history, excepting as far as regards the events which we have related, we shall leave our readers in the same state of uncertainty as were the inhabitants of Fort Louis; and although our'vocation and our sympathies naturally incline us to terra-firma, we must follow our hero for a few days in his adventurous course upon the ocean. The weather was as beautiful as it generally is on the western coast of France, at the commencement of autumn. The Indienne sailed gaily on with as fair a wind as could blow for her. The ship's crew, excepting those actually employed in manoeuvring the vessel, were availing themselves of the fine weather and occupied in their own matters, as caprice directed them, or were idly lounging about the ship, when all at once a voice which appeared to descend from the sky, called out, "Below, there!"

"Hullo, there!" replied the quarter-master, who was standing near the helm.

"Sail, ho!" cried the seaman who was on the lookout, at the head-mast.

"Sail, ho!" repeated the quarter-master. "Officer of the deck, be so good as to inform the captain there is a sail in sight."

"A sail! a sail!" re-echoed the crew from different parts of the deck; for at that moment a wave, having raised the vessel which appeared upon the horizon, had for an instant rendered her visible to the eyes of the ship's company.

"A sail!" exclaimed a young man of five-and-twenty, springing upon the quarter deck from the cabin stairs; "ask Mr Arthur what he thinks of her."

"Mast head, there!" cried the lieutenant, using his speaking trumpet; "the captain wants to know, Mr. Arthur, what you make of the strange sail."

Arthur, the young midshipman, had gone aloft immediately upon hearing a sail announced. He replied, "She looks like a large square-rigged vessel, close hauled, and steering for us."

"Yes, yes," said the young man, to whom Walter had given the title of captain, "she has as good eyes as we have, and she has seen us."

"Very well, if she wishes for a little chat, she will find us ready to talk to her. Besides, our guns must be almost choked from having their mouths stopped so long."

After some little time, the midshipman again hailed the officer on deck, and told him that the strange ship had just set her mainsail, and had altered her course a little, so as to cross their bow.

"Sir," said the captain, addressing the lieutenant, "get ready to beat to quarters, we must prepare for this fellow; he looks rather suspicious." And then calling out to the midshipman, "How does the ship seem to sail, Mr. Arthur? what do you think of her?"

"She seems to be a fast sailer, and is a man-of-war, I should think, by the squareness of her yards; and although I cannot see her flag, I would wager that she bears King George's commission."

"I should not wonder," observed the captain to the first lieutenant, "and that she has orders to give chase to a certain frigate called the Indienne, and that her commander is promised good promotion should he succeed in capturing her. Ha! ha! now she is loosing her top gallant sails. The blood hound has scented us, and is decidedly about to give us chase. Set our top gallant sails, too, Mr. Walter, and let us keep our course without varying a point. We shall see whether they will dare to come athwart our hawse."

The captain's orders were instantly repeated by the lieutenant, and in a few minutes the ship which had been running under her top sails, felt the influence of her top gallant sails, heeled over under this new pressure and bounded along as if animated by the sight of an enemy, and dashing away the spray from either bow with eager impetuosity.

For some time there was hardly a word uttered on board. Every one appeared to wait anxiously the termination of this state of suspense, and we shall profit by this momentary quiet, to call the attention of our readers to the person of the officer to whom the lieutenant had given the title of captain.

It was no longer either the young and sceptical lieutenant whom we have seen accompanying the Count d'Auray on board the ship, nor the old sea-wolf with his stooping gait, and harsh and snappish answers, who had received him in the cabin. He was a handsome young man, from twenty to twenty-five years of age, as we have said before, who, having thrown off all disguise, appeared at length in his own person, and dressed in the fanciful uniform which he always wore when upon the wide ocean. It was a sort of great coat of black velvet, with gold shoulder knots and fastened with hooks and eyes of the same metal. Round his waist he wore a Turkish belt, in which was placed a pair of elegant duelling pistols, richly inlaid and ornamented, apparently more for show than defence. His pantaloons were of white kerseymere, with boots which reached nearly to his knees. Round his neck, a cravat of transparent India muslin, embroidered with flowers in their natural colors, was loosely tied; his hair, no longer disfigured by powder, and black as ebony, flowed about his cheeks, which were tanned by exposure to the sun; his eyes beamed with hope and animation. Near him, upon a gun, was placed a steel helmet which fastened by a curb chain under the chin. This was his battle dress, and the only defensive armour which he wore. Some deep indentations in his helmet proved that it had more than once-saved the head which it protected from those severe wounds inflicted by those terrible cutlasses used by seamen when boarding. As to the ship's company, they wore the elegant though plain uniform of the French navy.

During this time, the vessel which had been described by the man at the mast head, and which had then appeared like a white speck upon the horizon, had become, little by little, a pyramid of sails and rigging. All eyes were fixed upon her, and although no order had been actually given, every one of the crew had taken the position which individually belonged to him, as though it had been determined that a combat should take place. There reigned then on board the Indienne that solemn and profound silence, which in a ship of war always precedes the decisive orders of the captain. Finally, the hull of the strange sail appeared rising out of the water, as her sails had successively done before. It was then clearly discernible that she was a larger ship than the Indienne, and that she carried thirty-six guns. She, however, showed no colors, and as her crew were carefully and completely concealed behind her bulwarks, it was impossible to ascertain, unless by some particular indications, to what nation she belonged. These two observations were made almost at the same moment by Captain Paul; the last, however, seemed to strike him the most forcibly.

"It appears," said he, addressing his lieutenant, "that we are going to have a scene of a masked ball. Order Arthur to bring us a few flags, and let us prove to this unknown, that the Indienne has several disguises at her disposal. And then, Mr. Walter, give orders that cutlasses and boarding pikes be distributed, for we can hardly expect, in these seas, to meet with any but enemy's ships."

The two orders were executed; as soon as given. In an instant the young midshipman had brought on deck a dozen flags of different nations, and Lieutenant Walter, having had the arm chest opened, had boarding pikes piled in different positions throughout the ship, and had distributed cutlasses and axes to the ship's company, he then returned to his place by the Captain's side. Every man again resumed his post by instinct rather than by order, for they had not yet beat to quarters; so that the apparent confusion which had existed for a moment ceased at once, and the frigate became once more, as it were, silent and attentive.

However, the two ships following their converging directions, continued to approach each other. When they were about the distance of three gun shots, "Mr. Walter," said the Captain, "I think it is time we should begin to mistify our good friend here. Let us show him the old Scotch flag."

The lieutenant gave a sign to the quartermaster, and the red Lion of Scotland, on a blue field, rose like a flame to the peak of the Indienne; but nothing on board the enemy's ship gave evidence of their paying the slightest attention to this manouvre.

"Yes, yes," murmured the captain, "the three leopards of England have so well filed the teeth and pared the claws of the Scottish lion, that they pay no attention to him, believing that he is tamed because he is defenceless. Show him some other color, Mr. Walter, and perhaps we shall succeed in loosening his tongue."

"What flag shall I hoist, captain?"

"Take the first one that comes; chance may perhaps favor us."

This order was scarcely given, when the Scotch flag was hauled down, and that of Sardinia took its place. The ship still remained mute.

"Well, well," said the captain, jestingly, "it appears that His Majesty, King George, is on good terms with his brother of Cyprus and Jerusalem. Do not let us bring them to loggerheads by carrying our joke farther, Mr. Walter, let us show the American flag, and prove that it is really the right one, by firing an unshotted gun."

The same manouvre was repeated. The Sardinian flag was hauled down, and the stars of the United States rose slowly towards the sky, and were certified by firing a gun.

What the captain had foreseen then happened immediately on the display of this symbol of rebellion rising insolently in the air. The unknown ship immediately betrayed its incognita by hoisting the British flag. At the same moment a cloud of smoke was seen issuing from the side of the royalist ship, and before the report was heard, a cannon ball was seen tipping from wave to wave, and fell about a hundred yards short of the Indienne.

"Beat to quarters, Mr. Walter, for you see we have guessed rightly. Come, my boys," cried he, to the crew, "hurrah for

America! and death to England!"

This was answered by a general shout, and had not ceased, when they heard them beating to quarters on board the Drake, for that was the name of the English ship. The drums of the Indienne immediately replied, and every man ran to his post:—the gunners to their guns, the officers to their stations, and the sailors to their running rigging. As to the captain, he jumped upon the top of the companion, his speaking trumpet in his hand—the supreme symbol, the sceptre of nautical royalty, which the commander always wields in the hour of combat or during the raging of the tempest.

They now seem to have made an exchange of parts, for the English appeared impatient, and the Americans affected calmness. The ships were hardly within gun shot, when a long line of smoke was seen issuing from the side of the English vessel, and a report similar to loud thunder was heard, and the iron messengers sent to deal death among the rebels, having in their impetuosity, miscalculated the distance, fell harmless before reaching the sides of the frigate. The latter, however, as if refusing to reply to so premature an attack, continued to haul to the wind, as if to spare the enemy too long a course.

At this moment the captain turned, as if to give a last look round his ship, and his astonished gaze was attracted by the appearance of a new personage on the deck, who had selected this dangerous and exciting moment to make his entrance upon the scene.

It was a young man, somewhere about twenty-two or

twenty-three years of age. His face was pale and mild; he was plainly, but elegantly dressed, and whom the captain had not before seen on board. He was leaning against the mizen-mast, his arms folded over his chest, and looking with melancholy indifference at the English vessel which was approaching them under a heavy press of canvas. The calmness at such a moment, and in a man who appeared a stranger to nautical combats, forcibly struck the captain. He then remembered the prisoner, whom the Count d'Auray had announced to him, and who had been brought on board during the last night he had passed at the anchorage of Port Louis.

"Who allowed you to come on deck, sir?" said he, softening as much as possible, the tone of his enquiry, so that it would have been difficult to ascertain whether this was addressed as a mere question, or as a reproach.

"No one, sir," replied the prisoner, in a soft and sorrowful voice; "but I had hoped that under the present circumstances, you would less severely observe the orders by which I became your prisoner."

"Have you forgotten that you were forbidden to hold any communication with the ship's company."

"I did not come here for the purpose of holding communication with the ship's company, sir; I came to see whether some friendly cannon ball would do me a good' turn."

"You may, but too soon, have your desire accomplished, if you remain where you are now standing; therefore, believe me, you had better remain below."

"Is this your advice; or an order, captain?"

"You have full liberty to construe it as you please."

"In that case," replied the young man, "I thank you—I will remain here."

At this instant, another loud report was heard; but the two ships had by this time neared each other so much, that they were within gun-shot, and the whole tempest of shot passed through the sails of the Indienne. Two splinters fell from the masts; and the groans and stifled cries of some of the ship's company were heard. The captain, at that moment, had his eyes fixed upon the prisoner, above whose head, a cannon ball had passed within two feet, grazing the mizen mast, against which he was leaning; but notwithstanding this death warning, he remained calm and unmoved, in the same attitude as if he had not felt the wing of the exterminating angel waft above his head. The captain knew how to appreciate courage—this incident was sufficient to assure him of the undaunted bravery of the man who stood before him.

"Tis well, sir," said he to him; "remain where you are, and when we come to boarding, if you should be tired of remaining with your arms crossed, take up a cutlass, or an axe, and give us a helping hand. You will excuse me not payings you more attention at this moment, for I have other things to do."

"Fire!" cried he, in a voice of thunder, through his speaking trumpet, "now, give it her: fire!"

"Fire!" repeated the officers like an echo, at their different stations.

At the instant, the Indienne trembled from her keel, to her royal mast head, as she poured her broadside into the enemy—a cloud of smoke spread itself like a veil, along the starboard-side, which was soon carried to leeward. The captain, standing upon the companion, impatiently awaited its clearing off, that he might ascertain the effect which the broadside had produced upon the enemy's vessel. When his gaze could penetrate through the smoke, he perceived that the enemy's main top mast had fallen, and had, with its sails, encumbered the after-part of the Drake's deck, and that her other sails were cut to ribbons. Then putting his speaking trumpet to his mouth, he cried—

"Well done! my lads. Now watch her closely. They will be too busy in clearing away the wreck of their mast, to think of raking us—fire—as you can—and this time shave close!"

The crew hastened to obey this order—the frigate veered round, and as the guns were brought to bear upon the enemy, they were discharged with terrible effect; and, as the captain had imagined, without any hindrance from the Drake. The Indienne once more trembled like a volcano, and, as a volcano, vomited forth her flame and smoke.

This time the gunners had followed the orders of their captain to the letter, (and the broadside had been fired point blank) striking the hull and the lower masts. Both her masts were still standing; but on all sides the sails were hanging in tatters. It appeared that some more considerable damage had been done, which it was impossible to ascertain at that distance; for some time, the broadside was not returned; at length it was, and instead of raking the Indienne, it struck her in a diagonal direction. It was not the less terrible, for it swept off many a brave fellow from the deck; but by a chance which appeared positively magical, touched neither of the masts. Some of the running rigging was cut, but nothing that prevented her manoeuvring as before. At one glance, Paul ascertained that he had only lost some men. His heart bounded with joy. He once more placed the speaking-trumpet to his mouth.

"Larboard the helm," cried he, "and board her on the larboard side! Boarders, to your stations—be ready! Give her one more broadside."

At the first movement of the Indienne, the enemy at once perceived the intention, and endeavoured to neutralize it by it similar movement, but at the instant of attempting to execute it, a dreadful crash was heard on board her, and the mainmast, which had been nearly cut through by the last discharge from the Indienne, trembled, for a few seconds like an uprooted tree, and fell forward, covering the deck with the mainsail and the rigging. Captain Paul at once comprehended what had delayed the return of the broadside.

"Now, she is ours, my lads!" cried he; "we have only to take her. One last broadside within pistol shot, and then we'll board her!"

The Indienne obeyed her helm, as does a well trained horse the bridle, and unopposed, advanced towards her enemy, for the latter had no steerage-way upon her, and her guns were consequently useless. The Drake was therefore at the mercy of her adversary, who by remaining at a distance and playing at long bowls, might have riddled her and sunk her, but disdaining this too easy victory, sent in a last broadside; and then, before seeing the effect it had produced, the frigate ran in upon her larboard quarter, and threw her grappling-irons on board. On the instant, the tops and forecastle of the Indienne blazed as with fireworks on a holiday, and flaming grenades were showered upon the deck of the Drake with the rapidity of hailstones.

"Courage, my lads, courage, lash the bowsprit to her quarter rails. Well done! now, to your two forecastle carronades—fire!"

All these orders were executed with magical celerity: the two ships were as securely lashed together as if by iron chains—the two carronades which had not been fired during the combat, thundered in there turn, and swept the enemy's deck with a cloud of grape shot, and then another cry was heard, uttered by the same stentorian voice—

"Now, board her!!!"

And, adding example to precept, the captain of the Indienne threw aside his speaking trumpet, now of no longer use, placed his helmet on his head, fastening the clasp beneath his chin; placed the sabre which he usually wore in his belt between his teeth, and rushed upon the bowsprit to jump thence upon the deck of the enemy.

Although this movement followed the order he had given with as great rapidity as the thunder succeeds the lightning, he was only the second upon the English deck:

he was preceded by the young prisoner with whom he had conversed, who had thrown aside his coat, and armed only with a hatchet, was the first to encounter death or victory.

"You are not conversant with the discipline of my ship," said Paul, laughing; "it is my place to be the first to board a ship I am attacking. I forgive you this time, but take care it does not again happen."

At the same instant, the seamen of the Indienne rushed from their own ship to the enemy's, taking advantage of every point of contact, some from the bowsprit, others from the end of the yards, and nettings, and fell upon the deck like ripe fruit falling from a tree when shaken by the wind. Then the English, who had retreated to their forecastle, unmasked a carronade which they had had time to turn upon their enemy. A volley of fire and iron was vomited forth on the assailants. One fourth of the crew of the Indienne fell killed or mutilated on the enemy's deck, in the midst of cries and maledictions. But above the cries and blasphemous oaths, a voice resounded, crying:

"Forward—all of you!"

Then ensued a scene of appalling confusion—a combat hand to hand—a general duel. To the roar of cannon, to the report of musketry, to the explosion of hand grenades, had succeeded the struggle with cold steel, less noisy but more sure, above all with seamen, who have retained for their sole use this inheritance from the giants, proscribed for more than two centuries on the field of battle. It was with hatchets that they cleaved each other's sculls; it was with cutlasses they wounded each other's breasts; it was with boarding-pikes that they nailed each other to the deck and masts. From time to time, in the midst of this mute carnage, a stray pistol shot was heard, but isolated, and as if ashamed of taking part in such a butchery. It lasted nearly a quarter of an hour, and amidst a confusion it would be impossible to describe. And then the British flag was lowered, and the crew of the Drake being driven below, there remained on deck only the conquerors, the wounded and the dead; in the midst of whom was the captain of the Indienne, surrounded by his crew, with his foot upon the breast of the captain of the enemy's ship, having on his right his first lieutenant, Walter, and on his left his young prisoner, whose shirt, steeped in blood, witnessed the share he had in the victory.

"Now, all is over," said Paul, stretching out his hand; "and he who strikes another blow will have to deal with me."

Then holding out his hand to his young prisoner, "Sir," said he, "you will relate to me, to-night, how it was that you were made my prisoner, will you not! For there must be some cowardly machination in this affair. The infamous only are transported to Cayenne, and you are too brave to be infamous."

CHAPTER IV.—THE MARCHIONESS.

She was a woman Of virtue most austere; noble in birth,
And of most royal presence—but sad thoughts
Seemed to possess her wholly—her children, even,
Seldom approached her, and when they did,
No soft affection, motherly caress,
Was e'er accorded to them—stern and cold,
She looked a moving statue.

—*Old Play.*

About six months after the occurrence of the events we have just related, and in the early part of the spring of 1780, a post chaise, whose wheels and panels covered with mud and dust, clearly certified that it had performed a long journey, was dragging slowly along, although two powerful horses were harnessed to it, upon the road between Vanness and Auray. The traveller it contained, and who was roughly jolted in traversing the cross-roads, was our former aquaintance, Count Emanuel, whom we saw open the scene upon the jetty of Fort Louis. He was coming from Paris with all haste, and proceeding to his ancient family mansion, with regard to which it is now necessary to give some more precise and circumstantial details.

Count Emanuel d'Auray was descended from one of the oldest families in Brittany—one of his ancestors had followed Saint Louis to the Holy Land, and from that time the name, of which he was the last inheritor, had been constantly blended with the history of our monarchy, whether in its victories or defeats. His father, the Marquis of d'Auray, Chevalier of the order of St. Louis, Commander of the order of St. Michael, and Grand Cross of the order of the Holy Ghost, enjoyed at the Court of Louis XV., in which he filled the post of high steward, that high distinction to which his birth, his fortune and nis personal merit, truly entitled him. His influence there had been increased by his marriage with Mademoiselle de Sable, who was his equal in every thing that regarded family or credit at court: so that a brilliant future was opened to the ambition of the young people, when, after being married five years, a report was suddenly spread about the court, that the Marquis d'Auray had become insane during a journey he had made to his estates. This report was for a long time disbelieved. At length the winter arrived, and neither the marquis nor his wife made their appearance at Versailles. His place was kept open for him another year, for the king, still hoping he would regain his reason, refused to appoint a successor to it; but a second winter passed on, and even the marchioness did not return to pay her court to the queen. In France people are soon forgotten; absence is a wearying malady, to which even the greatest names sooner or later must succumb. The shroud of indifference was gradually spread over this family, immured in their old chateau, as in a tomb, and whose voices were not heard either soliciting or complaining. Genealogists alone had duly enregistered the birth of a son and daughter, the only fruits of this union; the d'Aurays, therefore, continued to figure among the names of the French nobility; but not having mixed themselves up for more than twenty years either in court intrigues or in political affairs, not having sided either with a Pampadour or a Du Barry, not having distinguished themselves in the victories of the Maréchal de Broglie, or in the defeats of the Count Clermont—in short, having neither sound nor echo, they had been completely forgotten.

However, the ancient name of the lords of d'Auray had been twice pronounced at court, but without producing any impression. The first time on the occasion of the young Count Emanuel's being admitted in 1769, as one of the pages of Louis XV., and the second, when after having served his time as page, he entered the company of mousquetaires of the young King Louis XVI. He had, during this time, become acquainted with the Baron de Lectoure, a distant relation of M. de Maurepas, who was favorably disposed towards him, and who enjoyed a considerable degree of influence with that minister. Emanuel had been presented to his old courtier, who having been informed that the Count d'Auray had a sister, one day let fall a few words upon the possibility of an union between the two families. Emanuel, young and full of ambition, wearied with struggling beneath the veil which had obscured his family name, saw in this marriage a means of regaining the position which his father had occupied at court under the late king, and had eagerly caught at the first overtures for this alliance. M. de Lectoure, on his side, under the pretext of uniting himself still closer by the bands of brotherhood, to his young friend, had urged his suit with an eagerness which was so much the more flattering to Emanuel, that the man who demanded the hand of his sister had never seen her. The Marchioness d'Auray had listened the more readily to this proposal, as it opened to her son the road to royal favor, and the marriage was agreed upon, if not between the two young people, at all events between the families. Emanuel, who preceded M. de Lectoure three or four days only, had hastened into the country to inform his mother that everything had been arranged according to her desire. As to Marguerite, the intended wife, they contented themselves with informing her of the resolution they had taken without thinking it necessary to ask her consent to it, in about the same way that a criminal is informed of the sentence which condemns him to the scaffold.

It was, therefore, thus cradling himself in the brilliant dreams of future exalted favor, and bouying himself up with the most elevated projects of ambition, that young Count Emanuel re-entered the gloomy castle of his family, whose feudal towers, black walls, and court yards, overgrown with grass, formed so striking a contrast with the golden hopes that agitated him. The castle was a league and a half distant from any other dwelling. The principal facade overlooked that part of the ocean, which being so constantly swept by storms, has obtained the name of "the Wild Sea." The other looked toward an immense park, which, being for twenty years abandoned and uncultivated, had become a complete forest. As to the apartments, they had remained constantly closed, with the exception of those inhabited by the family.

The furniture, which had been renewed during the reign of Louis XIV., had, thanks to the care of a numerous household, retained a rich and aristocratic appearance, which the more modern part of it had begun to lose, and which, although more elegant, was less magnificent. It had been supplied from the workshops of Boule, the appointed upholsterer of the court.

It was into one of these rooms, with deep mouldings, sculptured chimney pieces, and ceiling painted in fresco, that the Count Emanuel was ushered on alighting from his carriage. He was in such haste to communicate to his mother the happy news of which he was the bearer, that without taking the time to change his dress, he threw his hat, his gloves, and travelling pistols on the table, and ordered an old servant to inform the marchioness of his arrival, and to ask her permission to present himself, saying that he would await it in that room; for such in this old family was the respect paid to parents, that the son, after an absence of five months, did not dare to present himself to his mother, without in the first place consulting her desires upon the subject. As to the Marquis d'Auray, his children could not remember having seen him more than two or three times, and then it was by stealth: for his insanity was of a nature, it was said, that certain objects irritated, and they had been always kept from him with the greatest precaution. The marchioness alone, a model of conjugal virtue, remained always with him, fulfilling towards the poor lunatic not only the duties of a wife, but also those of a servant. Consequently, her name was revered in the surrounding villages, as that of a saint, whose devotedness on earth has gained a place in heaven.

In a few moments the old servant returned, and announced that the marchioness d'Auray preferred coming down to him, and begged that the count would wait for her in the room in which he then was. Almost immediately afterward the door of the room again opened, and Emanuel's mother entered it. She was about forty or forty-five years of age, tall and pale, but still handsome, whose calm, austere and melancholy features had a singular appearance of haughtiness, energy, and command. She was in costume of a widow as adopted in 1760, for since the time that her husband had lost his reason, she had never laid aside her mourning garments. Her long black gown gave to her movements, cold and slow as those of a shadow, a solemn appearance, which shed around this extraordinary woman a feeling of awe, which even filial affection had never been able to surmount. Therefore, on seeing her, Emanuel started as at the sight of an unexpected apparition, and instantly rising, he advanced three steps toward her, respectfully went down upon one knee, and kissed the hand she presented to him.

"Rise, sir," said the marchioness. "I am happy to see you again." And she pronounced these words with as little emotion as if her son, who had been absent five months, had left her but the day before. Emanuel obeyed, conducted his mother to a large arm chair, in which she seated herself, and he remained standing before her.

"I received your letter, count," she said, "and I congratulate you on your skill. You appear to me born for diplomacy, and even more so than for military life. You ought to request the Baron de Lectoure to obtain an embassy for you, rather than a regiment."

"Lectoure is ready to solicit any thing we may desire, madam; and what is more, he will obtain any thing we may solicit, so great is his power with M. Maurepas, and so great is his love for my sister."

"In love with a woman he has never seen?"

"Lectoure is a gentleman, madam, and the portrait I have drawn of Marguerite, and perhaps the information he has received as to our fortune, has inspired him with the most earnest desire to become your son and to call himself my brother. And therefore he has requested that all the preliminary ceremonies may be gone through in his absence. You have obtained the publication of the bans, madam?"

"Yes."

"The day after to-morrow, then, the marriage contract can be signed."

"With the help of God, all will be ready."

"Thanks, madam."

"But tell me," continued the marchioness, leaning on the arm of her chair, and bending toward Emanuel, "has he not questioned you regarding that young man, for whom he obtained from the minister an order of deportation?"

"By no means, my mother, these are services which are asked without entering into any explanation, and which are granted in implicit confidence. It is well understood between people who know the world, that they are to be forgotten as soon as rendered."

"Then he knows nothing?"

"No—but did he know all——"

"Well?"

"Well, madam, I believe he is so much of a philosopher, that the discovery would not in any way influence his determination."

"I thought as much; he is a ruined spendthrift," replied the marchioness, with an indescribable expression of contempt, and as if speaking to herself.

"But supposing it should be so," said Emanuel anxiously, "your resolution would be still unchanged, I hope."

"Are we not rich enough to repair his fortune if he can restore our former influence?"

"Then, there is only my sister——"

"Do you doubt that she will obey me, when I inform her of my will?"

"Can you believe, then, that she has forgotten Lusignan?"

"For seven months, at least, she has not dared to remember him in my presence."

"Reflect, my mother, that this marriage is the only means by which our family can be restored to influence; for there is one thing I must not conceal from you. My father has been ill for fifteen years, and having been absent from court so long, was completely forgotten by the old king at his death, and by the young king on his accession to the throne. Your virtuous attention to the marquis, has not permitted you to leave him, even for a moment, since the hour in which he was deprived of reason; your virtues, madam, are of that nature which God sees, and recompenses, but of which the world remains ignorant; and while you are fulfilling in this old forgotten castle in Brittany, the holy and consolatory mission, which you call a duty, your former friends disappear, they die, or they forget you (this is a painful truth to people, who like us, can count six hundred years of illustrious nobility); for when I reappeared at court, our name, the name of the family d'Auray, was hardly known to their majesties, but as an historical recollection."

"Yes; I know full well that kings have but short memories," murmured the marchioness; but instantly, and as if reproaching herself for such a blasphemy, she rejoined, "I hope that the blessing of God may always attend their majesties and France."

"And what can in any way affect their happiness?" replied Emanuel, with that perfect confidence in the future, which in those days was the distinctive, characteristic of the hair-brained and unthinking nobility. "Louis XVI. is young and good; Marie Antoinette young and lovely; both of them beloved by a brave and loyal people. Fate has placed them, Heaven be praised, beyond the reach of every evil."

"No one, my son," replied the marchioness, mournfully shaking her head, "believe me, is placed beyond the reach of human woes and human frailty. No heart, however confidently its owner may believe that he can master it, firm as it may be, is proof against the passions; and no head, were it even a crowned one, but may be blanched in a single night. The people, you say, are brave and loyal." The marchioness arose and slowly advanced to the window, and with a solemn gesture pointing to the ocean. "Observe that sea; it is now calm and peaceful; and yet to-morrow, this night, in an hour perhaps, the breath of the tempest may bear us the cries of distress of unhappy beings it is about to engulph. Although I am separated from the world, strange reports sometimes reach my ears, borne as it were by invisible and prophetic spirits. Does there not exist a sect of philosophers which has led away men of high name, by the errors which it propagates? Do they not speak of a whole world, which is detaching itself from the mother country, whose children refuse to acknowledge their father? Is there not a people who style themselves a nation? Have I not heard it said that men of high birth have crossed the ocean, to offer to rebels, swords which their ancestors never drew but at the call of their legitimate sovereigns? and have I not been told, moreover, or is it but the dream of my solitude, that King Louis XVI. and the Queen, Marie Antoinette herself, forgetting that sovereigns are a family of brothers, have authorised these armed emigrations, and have given letters of marque to I know not what foreign pirate?"

"All this is true," said Emanuel, much astonished.

"May God, then, watch over their majesties, the King and Queen of France!" rejoined the marchioness as she slowly retired from the room, leaving Emanuel so astounded at these painful forebodings, that he saw her withdraw without uttering a word or even making a gesture to retain her.

Emanuel remained for some time pensive and serious, but soon his buoyant character surmounted these gloomy presages, and as if thinking to change his ideas by changing the view he had been gazing at, he left the window which opened towards the sea, and crossed the room to another, whence he could discern the whole of the plain which extends itself between d'Auray and Vannes. He had been there but a few minutes, when he perceived two persons on horseback, following the same road he had just travelled over, and who appeared to be approaching the castle. As they drew nearer he could distinguish that they were a gentleman and his servant. The first, dressed in the costume of young men of fashion of that day, that is to say, in a short green riding coat with gold frogs, stocking-knit breeches, and top-boots, wearing a round hat with a broad brim, and his hair tied with a large bow of ribbons. He was mounted on an English horse of rare beauty and great value, which he managed with a grace that proved he had made equestrian exercises a profound study. He was followed at a short distance by a servant, whose aristocratic livery was in perfect harmony with the lordly air of the person whom he served. Emanuel imagined for a moment on seeing them proceed so directly towards the castle, that it was the Baron de Lectoure, who, having hastened his departure from Paris, intended to surprise him; but he soon found that he was mistaken; and although it appeared to him that it was not the first time he had seen the horseman, he could not recollect where or under what circumstances he had met him.

While he was racking his memory to discover the event in his life with which this vague remembrance was connected, the strangers had disappeared behind an angle of the castle wall. Five minutes afterwards Emanuel heard the sound of their horses' feet in the court yard, and, almost immediately the door was opened; a servant announced, "Mr. Paul!"

CHAPTER V.—DEVOTED LOVE.

Woman's love
Once given, may break the heart that holds—but never
Melts into air save with her latest sigh.
Bulwer.—The Sea Captain,

The name, as well as the appearance of the person thus announced, awakened in their turn in the mind of Emanuel a confused recollection of which he could not affix either date or event. The person, preceded by the servant, entered the room by a door opposite the one through which the marchioness had retired. Although the moment was ill-timed for a visit, and though the young count, pre-occupied by his projects for the future, would have preferred meditating upon and ripening them, he was compelled, by the rules of etiquette, so severe in those days between well-bred people, to receive the visitor with courtesy and politeness. The deportment of the latter bespoke the man of distinction. After the usual salutations, Emanuel, by a gesture, invited the stranger to be seated, who bowed and took a chair, and then the conversation commenced with some common-place polite observation.

"I am delighted to meet you, count," said the stranger.

"Chance has favored me, sir," replied Emanuel; "an hour sooner you would not have found me here: I have just arrived from Paris."

"I am aware of that, count, for we have been travelling the same road. I set out an hour after you, and all along the road I heard of you, by means of the postillions who had the honor of driving you."

"May I be bold enough to ask," said Emanuel, in a tone which began to evince a certain degree of dissatisfaction, "to what circumstance I owe the interest you appear to evince concerning me."

"This interest is perfectly natural between old acquaintance, and perhaps. I might have reason to complain that it does not appear to be reciprocal."

"In fact, sir, it does appear to me," replied Emanuel, "that I have met you somewhere; but my recollection serves me but confusedly; will you be kind enough to assist it?"

"If what you say be the case, count, your memory must indeed be rather fugitive, for within the last six months, on three separate occasions, I have the honor of exchanging compliments with you."

"Even should I expose myself to further reproach, I am compelled to say that I still remain in the same state of uncertainty with regard to your person. Pray, therefore, have the goodness to fix my memory, by aid of more precise dates, on some event, and remind me under what circumstances I had the honor of meeting you for the first time."

"The first time, count? it was on the jetty of Port Louis. You desired to obtain some information with regard to a certain frigate, which I was so fortunate as to be able to furnish you. I believe, even, that I accompanied you on board. Upon that occasion I wore the uniform of a lieutenant in the royal navy, and you that of a mousquetaire."

"I now well recollect it, sir, and I was obliged to leave the vessel without offering the thanks I owed you."

"You are mistaken, count; I received those thanks during our second interview."

"And where did that take place?"

"On board the very vessel to which I had conducted you—in the cabin. I then wore the uniform of the captain of the ship: blue coat, red waistcoat and breeches, with grey stockings, a three-cornered hat, and curled hair. Only the captain appeared to you some thirty years older than the lieutenant, and it was not without motive that I had made myself appear so much older, for you would perhaps, not have chosen to confide to a young man a secret of such importance as you then communicated to me."

"What you now say is incredible, sir; and yet something tells me that it was really so. Yes, yes; I now remember that in the shade in which you remained half concealed, I saw eyes sparkling similar to yours. I have not forgotten them; but this was only the time before the last, you say, that I had the honor of seeing you. Continue, sir, I beg, to assist my memory, for I cannot recollect our third interview."

"The last, count, was only a week since, at Paris—at a fencing match, at Saint-George's, in the rue Chanterecin. You remember, do you not, an English gentleman, with his hair so red that his powder could scarcely conceal its brilliant color—a scarlet coat, and tightly fitting pantaloons. I even had the honor of trying a bout with you, and I was fortunate enough to hit you three times, while, on the contrary, you were not lucky enough to touch me once. On that occasion I called myself Jones."

"It is most singular—it was certainly the same look, but it could not be the same man."

"The will of God has directed that the look should be the only thing which cannot be disguised, and this is why he has thrown into the look a spark of his own light. Well, then, the lieutenant, the captain, the Englishman, were one and the same person."

"At the present moment, sir, what are you if you please? For, with a man who can so perfectly disguise himself, that question you must admit, is not altogether unnecessary."

"At the present moment, count, as you see, I have no motive for concealment, and, therefore, I have come to you in the simple costume of the young nobility, when they visit each other as neighbors in the country. I am whatever you may please to consider me; French, English, Spanish, or even an American. In which of these languages would you wish our conversation to be continued?"

"Although some of these languages may be as familiar to me as they are to you, sir, I prefer the French language; it is that of a plain and concise explanations."

"Be it so," replied Paul, with an expression of profound melancholy; "the French is also the language I prefer; I first saw the day upon French ground, for the sun of France was that which gladdened my eyes; and although I have often seen more fertile climes, and a more brilliant sun, there has never been for me but one country and one sun, the sun and the country of Franco!"

"Your national enthusiasm," said Emanuel, interrupting him ironically, "causes you to forget the motive to which I am indebted for the honor of this visit."

"You are right, sir, and I will return to it. It was, then, about six months ago, while walking on the jetty of Port Louis, you saw in the outer roads a fine sharp frigate, with tall masts and square yards, and you said to yourself: 'the captain of that ship must have some motive known only to himself, for carrying so much canvas, on masts so slight,'—and from that sprung to your mind that he must be some buccaneer, a pirate, a corsair"——

"And was I mistaken?"

"I thought I had already expressed to you, count," replied Paul, with a slight tone of irony, "my admiration of the perspicacity with which, at the first glance, you sound the depths of men and circumstances"——

"A truce to compliments, if you please, sir, and let us to facts."

"It was under this persuasion that you caused yourself to be conducted on board the frigate, by a certain lieutenant, and that you found a certain captain in the cabin. You were the bearer of a letter from the Minister of Marine, ordering any officer, upon your requisition, and whose ship was under the French flag and bound for the Gulf of Mexico, to conduct to Cayenne a person named Lusignan, guilty of a crime against the state."

"That is true."

"I obeyed that order, for I was then ignorant that this great culprit, thus transported, had committed no other crime than that of being the lover of your sister."

"Sir," cried Emanuel, starting up.

"These are very fine pistols, count," carelessly continued Paul, playing with the weapons which the Count d'Auray had placed upon the table, on alighting from his carriage.

"And they are ready loaded," said Emanuel, in a tone which was not to be mistaken.

"Are they so?" returned Paul, with affected indifference.

"That is a matter of which you can assure yourself, if you will take a turn in the park with me."

"There is no necessity for going out to do that," replied Paul, without pretending to understand Emanuel's proposal in the sense which he meant to give to it; "here is a mark which is well placed, and at a proper distance."

Saying these words, the captain cocked the pistol, and pointed it through the open window towards the top of a small tree. A goldfinch was rocking himself on the highest branch, singing forth his shrill and joyful notes. Paul fired, and the poor bird, cut in two, fell at the foot of the tree. Paul coolly replaced the pistol on the table.

"You were perfectly right, count," said he, "they are excellent weapons, and I advise you not to part with them."

"You have just given me an extraordinary proof of it," replied Emanuel; "and I feel bound to acknowledge that you have a steady hand."

"There is nothing extraordinary in that," rejoined Paul,

in that melancholy tone which was peculiar to him. "During those long days, when not a breath passes over that mirror of the Supreme Being, which is called the ocean, we seamen are compelled to seek for amusements to which you landsmen are daily accustomed. Then we try our skill upon the sea-gulls, which hover over the crest of a wave; or the fish-hawks, which dart down upon the imprudent tenant of the deep that rise to its surface; or, again, upon the swallows which, fatigued with a long flight, alight upon the royal mast-head or on the yards or rigging. It is thus, count, that we acquire some dexterity in exercises which may appear so incompatible with our profession."

"Go on, sir; and if it be possible, let us return to the subject of our conversation."

"He was a handsome, brave young man, this Lusignan; he related his whole history to me. That being the son of an old friend of your father's, who had died poor, he had been adopted by him some two years before the unknown accident occurred which deprived him of his reason. That having been brought up with you, he had inspired you with hatred—your sister with affection. He told me that, during the long years they passed together in the same solitude, they never perceived the isolation from the world in which they lived, excepting when they were absent from each other. He recounted to me all the details of their youthful love, and how Marguerite had one day said to him, in the words of the tender maiden of Verona—

"'I will be thine, or else I'll be the tomb's.'"

"She has but too truly kept her word."

"Yes—has she not? And you virtuous people call that shame and dishonour, when a poor child, lost through her own innocence, is carried away by love. Your mother, whose duties estranged her from her daughter, and perpetually confined her to your father's room—(for I know the virtues of your mother, sir, as well as I know your sister's weakness: she is an austere woman, more severe than one of God's creatures ought to be, whose only advantage over others is, that of never having fallen)—your mother, I say, one night heard some stifled cries; she entered your sister's chamber, walked pale and silently up to her bed, and coldly snatched from her arms a child which had just been born, and left the room without addressing even a reproach to her daughter, but only paler and more silent than when she entered it. As to poor Marguerite, she did not utter even a cry—she made no complaint. She had fainted away immediately on perceiving her mother. Was it so, sir? Have I been rightly informed, and is the whole of this dreadful story true?"

"You seem to be acquainted with every detail of it!" exclaimed Emanuel, with amazement.

"It is because the whole of these details are given in these letters signed by your sister," replied Paul, opening a pocket-book, "and which Lusignan, at the time he was about to be thrown amid robbers and assassins, through your instrumentality, confided to me, that I might restore them to her who had written them."

"Give them to me, then," said Emanuel, stretching

forth his hand towards the pocket-book, "and they shall be faithfully delivered to her who has had the imprudence"—

"To complain to the only person who loved her in this world—is it not so?" said Paul, withdrawing the letters and the pocket-book. "Imprudent daughter, whose own mother snatched the child from her heart, and who poured her bitter tears into the bosom of the father of her child! Imprudent sister, who, not finding any protection from this tyranny in her brother, has compromised his noble name by signing with the name he bears, letters, which, in the stupid and prejudiced eye of the world, may—how is it you term this in your noble class—dishonour her family, is it not?"

"Then," cried Emanuel, reddening with impatience, "since you are aware of the terrible tendency of these papers, fulfil the mission which you have been charged, by delivering them either to me, to my mother, or my sister."

"This was my intention when I landed at Lorient; but about ten or twelve days ago, on entering a church—"

"A church!"

"Yes, sir."

"And for what purpose?"

"To pray there."

"Ah! Captain Paul believes in God, then!"

"Did I not believe in him, whom should I invoke during the raging of the tempest?"

"And in this church, then?"

"In that church, sir, I heard a priest announce the approaching marriage of the noble Marguerite d'Auray with the very high and very potent Baron de Lectoure. I immediately inquired for you, and was informed you were at Paris, where I was myself compelled to go, to give an account of my mission to the king."

"To the king!"

"Yes, sir, to the king—Louis XVI.; to his majesty, in person. I immediately set out, intending to return here as soon as you did. I met you in Saint George's rooms, and was informed of your approaching departure. I arranged mine in consequence, in order that we might arrive here at about the same time, and here I am, sir, with a very different resolution to that I had formed before landing in Brittany."

"And what is this new determination? Let me hear it, for we must come to some conclusion."

"Well, then, I think that as all the world, and even his mother, seem to have forgotten the poor orphan, it is highly necessary that I should remember it. In the position in which you are placed, sir, and with the disposition you have evinced of becoming allied to the Baron de Lectoure (who in your view, is the only person who can assist the realization of your ambitious projects), these letters are well worth a hundred thousand francs, are they not? and will make but a very trifling breach in the income of two hundred thousand francs which your estates afford you."

"But who will prove to me that this hundred thousand francs—"

"You are right, sir, and therefore it will be in exchange for a contract for an annuity upon the young Hector de

Lusignan, that I will deliver up these letters."

"Is that all, sir?"

"I will also ask, that the child be confided to me, and I will have him brought up, thanks to his little fortune, far from the mother who has forgotten him, and far from his father whom you caused to be banished."

"'Tis well, sir; had I known that it was for so small a sum, and so trifling an interest that you had come, I should not have experienced so much anxiety. You will, however, permit me to speak to my mother on the subject."

"Monsieur le Comte," said a servant, opening the door.

"I am not at home to any one. Leave the room." replied Emanuel, impatiently.

"It is your sister, sir, who wishes to see you."

"Tell her to come by and by."

"She desires to speak to you this instant."

"Do not put yourself out of the way on my account," said Paul.

"But my sister must not see you, sir,—you comprehend it is important that she should not see you."

"As you please; but as it is important, also, that I should not leave the castle before concluding the affair which brought me here, permit me to go into this side room."

"That will do," said Emanuel, himself opening the door; "but be quick, I beg of you."

Paul went into the small room, and Emanuel hastily closed the door upon him, which was hardly done when Marguerite appeared.

CHAPTER VI. BROTHER AND SISTER.

Look kindly on them; I cannot bear Severity;
My heart's so tender, should you charge me rough,
I should but weep and answer you with sobbing;
But use me gently, like a loving brother,
And search through all the secrets of my soul.

—*Otway.*

Marguerite d'Auray, whose history the reader has become aquainted with, from the conversation between Captain Paul and Emanuel, was one of those delicate, pale beauties, who bear impressed upon their features the characteristic stamp of high birth. At the first glance, from the soft flexibility of her form, the whiteness of her skin, the shape of her hands and tapering fingers, with their thin, rosy and transparent nails, could be discerned that she was descended from an ancient race. It was evident that her feet, so small that both of them could have been placed in the foot-mark of most women, had never walked excepting on carpeted saloons or on the flowery turf of a park. There was in her movements, graceful as they were, a certain degree of haughtiness and pride, the attribute of all her family; in fine, she conveyed the impression that her soul, capable of making any sacrifice she had resolved upon, was very likely to rebel against tyranny; that devotedness was an instinctive virtue of her heart, while obedience, in her view, was only an educational duty, so that the tempest wind which blew upon her, might make her bend down before it as a lily, but not as a reed.

And yet, when she appeared at the door, her features depicted such complete discouragement, her eyes had retained the traces of such burning tears, her whole frame seemed weighed down by such an overwhelming despair, that Emanuel saw at once, that she must have summoned all her strength to assume an appearance of calmness. On seeing him, she made a violent effort, and it was with a certain degree of nervous firmness that she approached the arm chair on which he was sitting. And then, seeing that the features of her brother retained the expression of impatience, which they had assumed on being interrupted, she paused, and these two children of the same mother, looked at each other as strangers, the one with the eyes of ambition, the other with those of fear. By degrees, Marguerite resumed her courage.

"You have come at last, Emanuel! I was awaiting your return as the blind await the light, and yet from the manner in which you look upon your sister, it is easy to perceive that she was wrong in placing her hopes in you."

"If my sifter has become, as she always ought to have been," replied Emanuel, "that is to say, a submissive and respectful daughter, she will have understood what her rank and her position demand of her; she will have forgotten past events as things which never should have happened, and which consequently she ought not to remember, and she will have prepared herself for the new destiny which awaits her.

If it is in this disposition that she now comes before me, my arms are open to receive her, and my sister is still my sister."

"Listen attentively to what I am about to say," said Marguerite, "and above all, consider it as a justification of myself, and not intended as a reproach to others. If my mother—and God forbid that I should accuse her, for a holy duty keeps her apart from us—if my mother had been, I was about to say, toward me as other mothers are towards their daughters, I should constantly have opened my heart to her as a book; at the first word traced upon it by any stranger hand, she would have warned me of my danger and I should have avoided it. Had I been educated in the world instead of being brought up like a poor wild flower beneath the shade of this old castle, I should have learned from infancy the value of the rank and position which you speak of to-day, and I should, perhaps, not have infringed the decorum they prescribe, or the duties they impose. In short, had I been tutored amidst women of the world, with their sparkling wit and frivolous hearts, whom I have so often heard you praise, but whom I never knew, had I been guilty of some faults from levity, which love has caused me to commit—yes, I can well understand, I might then have forgotten the past, have sown upon the surface new recollections as flowers are planted upon tombs; and then, forgetting the place where they had grown, have formed of them a bouquet for a ball, or a bridal wreath. But unfortunately it is not so, Emanuel. I was told to beware, when it was too late to avoid the danger. They spoke to me of my rank and position in society, when I had already forfeited them, and I am now called upon to look forward to joy in the future, when my heart is drowned in the tears and misery of the past."

"And the conclusion of all this,"bitterly rejoined Emanuel.

"The conclusion depends on you alone, Emanuel; it is in your power to render it, if not happy, at all events becoming. I cannot have recourse to my father. Alas! I know not even if he could recognise his daughter. I have no hope in my mother; her glance freezes me, her words are death to me. You alone, Emanuel, were left to me, to whom I could say, brother: you are now the head of the family; it is to you alone that we are answerable for our honor. I have fallen from ignorance, and I have been punished for my fault as if it had been a wilful crime."

"Well! well!", murmured Emanuel impatiently, "what is it that you ask?"

"Brother, I demand, since a union with the only being I could have loved, is said to be impossible, I demand that my punishment be regulated according to my strength to bear it. My mother—may heaven pardon her!—tore my child from me as if she had never herself been a mother, and my child will be brought up far from me, neglected, and in obscurity. You, Emanuel, removed the father, as my mother did the child, and you were more cruel to him than the case required; I will not say as man to man, but even as a judge towards a guilty person. As to myself, you have both united to impose upon me a martyrdom more painful still. Well, then, Emanuel, I demand in the name of our childhood spent in the same cradle, of our youth passed under the same roof, in the name of the tender appellations of brother and sister, which nature bestowed upon us—I demand that a convent be opened to me, and that its gates should close upon me for ever. And in that convent, I swear to you, Emanuel, that every day upon my knees, before God, my forehead bent down to the stone-pavement, weighed down by my fault, I will entreat the Lord as a recompense for all my sufferings, to restore my father to reason, my mother to happiness, and to pour on you, Emanuel, honor, and glory and fortune. I swear to you, I will do this."

"Yes; and the world will say that I had a sister whom I sacrificed to my fortune, whose property I inherited while she still lived! Why this is sheer madness!"

"Listen to me, Emanuel," rejoined Marguerite, supporting herself on the back of a chair, near which she was standing.

"Well?" replied Emanuel.

"When you have pledged your word, you keep it, do you not?"

"I am a gentleman."

"Well, then! look at this bracelet."

"I see it—perfectly—what then?"

"It is fastened by a key—the key which opens it is attached to a ring, and with that ring, I pledged my word that I would not be released from a promise I had made, until the ring should be brought back and returned to me."

"And he who has the key of it?"

"Thanks to you, and to my mother, Emanuel, he is too far

from us to ask it of him. He is at Cayenne."

"Before you are married two months," replied Emanuel, with an ironical smile, "that bracelet will be so irksome to you, that you will be the first to get rid of it."

"I thought that I had told you it is locked upon my arm."

"You know what people do when they have lost the key and cannot get into their house—they send for a locksmith."

"Well! in my case, Emanuel," replied Marguerite, rasing her voice, and extending her arm with a solemn gesture, "they must send for the executioner then, for this hand shall be cut off before I give it to another."

"Silence! silence!" cried Emanuel, rising hastily, and looking anxiously towards the door of the inner room.

"And now I have said all I had to say," rejoined Marguerite: "my only hope was in you, Emanuel; for although you cannot comprehend any deep-seated feeling, you are not cruel. I came to you in tears, look at me and you will see that it is true—I came to you to say, 'Brother, this marriage is the misfortune, is the misery of my life—I would prefer a convent—I would prefer death to it—and you have not listened to me, or if you have listened, you have not understood me. Well, then, I will address myself to this man—I will appeal to his honor, to his delicacy; if that should not be sufficient, I will tell him all; my love for another, my weakness, my fault, my crime! I will tell him that I have a child; that although he was torn from me, although I have never since seen him, although I am ignorant of his abode, still my child exists. A child cannot die, without his death striking some chord within its mother's heart. In short I will tell him, should it be necessary, that I still love another, that I cannot love him, and that I never will."

"Well! tell him all this," cried Emanuel, irritated by her persistence, "and that evening we will sign the contract, and the next day you will be Baroness de Lectoure."

"And then," replied Marguerite, "then, I shall be truly the most miserable woman in existence, for I should then have a brother whom I should no longer love, and a husband for whom I should have no esteem. Farewell, Emanuel; believe me this contract is not yet signed."

And after saying these words, Marguerite withdrew with that deep and settled despair upon her features, which could not for a moment be mistaken. And Emanuel, convinced that he had not, as he had anticipated, obtained a victory, but that the struggle was still to be continued, gazed after her with an anxiety which was not devoid of tenderness.

After a few moments of silence, in which he sat pensive and motionless, he turned round and saw Captain Paul, whom he had completely forgotten, standing at the door of the study, and then considering the vital importance it was to him to get possession of the papers, which the captain had offered him, he hurriedly sat down at the table, took a pen and paper, and turning towards him, said—

"And now, sir, we are again alone, and there is nothing to prevent our at once concluding this affair. In what terms do you wish the promise to be drawn up? Dictate them, I am ready to write them down."

"It is now useless," coldly replied the captain.

"And why so?"

"I have changed my mind."

"How is that?" said Emanuel, rising, alarmed at the consequences which he perceived might arise from words which he was far from expecting.

"I will give," replied Paul, with the calmness of a fixed determination, "the hundred thousand livres to the child, and I will find a husband for your sister."

"Who are you, then," said Emanuel, advancing a step towards him, "who are you, sir, who thus disposes of a young girl who is my sister, who has never seen you, and who does not even know that you exist?"

"Who am I!" replied Paul, smiling; "upon my honor, I know no more upon that subject than you do, for my birth is a secret which is only to be revealed to me when I have attained my twenty-fifth year."

"And you will attain that age?"——

"This evening, sir. I place myself at your disposal from to-morrow morning, to give you all the information you may require of me," and saying these words, Paul bowed.

"I allow you to depart, sir, but you will understand it is upon the condition that we meet again."

"I was about to propose that condition, count, and I thank you for having anticipated me."

He then bowed to Emanuel a second time, and left the room. At the castle gate, Paul found his horse and servant, and resumed the route to Port Louis. When he had got out of sight of the castle, he alighted from his horse, and directed his steps towards a fisherman's hut, built upon the beach. At the door of this house, seated upon a bench, and in a sailor's' dress, was a young man so deeply absorbed in thought, that he did not observe Paul's approach. The captain placed his hand upon the young man's shoulder, the other started, looked at him, and became frightfully pale, although the open and joyful countenance of Paul, indicated that he was far from being the bearer of bad news.

"Well!" said Paul to him, "I have seen her."

"Who?" demanded the young man.

"Marguerite, by heaven!"

"And——"

"She is charming."

"I did not ask you that."

"She loves you still."

"Gracious heaven!" exclaimed the young man, throwing himself into Paul's arms, and bursting into tears.

CHAPTER VII.—THE FAITHFUL SERVANT.

O good old man; how well in thee appears
The constant service of the antique world
When service sweat for duty, not for need!

Thou art not for the fashion of these times
Where none will sweat but for promotion;
And having that, do choice their service up
Even with the having: it is not so with thee.

Shakespeare.

Although our readers must readily comprehend, after that which we have just related to them, all that had passed in the six months during which we had lost sight of our heroes, some details are, however, necessary, in order that they should fully understand the new events about to be accomplished.

On the evening after the combat between the Indienne and the Drake, and which, notwithstanding our ignorance in naval matters, we have attempted to describe to our readers, Lusignan had related to Paul the history of his whole life. It was a very simple one, and contained but few incidents. Love had formed the principal event in it, and after having been its only joy, it had become its greatest grief. The adventurous and independent life of Paul, his station, which had placed him beyond the trammels of society, his caprice which was superior to all laws, his habit of supreme command on board his own ship, had inspired him with too just a sense of natural rights to obey the order he had received with regard to Lusignan. Moreover, although he had anchored under the French flag, Paul, as we have seen, belonged to the navy of America, whose cause he had enthusiastically espoused. He continued, therefore, his cruise along the shores of England; but finding there was nothing to be done on the sea he landed at Whitehaven, a small port in Cumberland, at the head of twenty men, among whom was Lusignan, took the fort, spiked the guns, and put to sea again, after having burnt the merchant vessels in the roads. Thence he sailed for the coast of Scotland, with the intention of carrying off the Earl of Selkirk and taking him as a hostage to the United States; but this project had miscarried from an unforeseen circumstance, that nobleman having unexpectedly gone to London. In this enterprise, as in the other, Lusignan had seconded him with the courage we have seen him exhibit in the battle between the Indienne and the Drake; so that Paul congratulated himself more than ever upon the chance which had enabled him to oppose an injustice. But it was not enough that he had saved Lusignan from transportation, it was necessary to restore his honor, and to our young adventurer, in whom our readers will doubtless have recognised the celebrated privateersman, Paul Jones, it was a more easy matter than to any other person; for having letters of marque from Louis XVI., against the English, he had to repair to Versailles to give an account of his cruize.

Paul determined upon running into Lorient, and for the

second time cast anchor there, that he might be within a short distance of the Chateau d'Auray. The first answer which the young men received to their enquiries regarding that family, was that Marguerite d'Auray was about to be married to M. do Lectoure. Lusignan thought himself' forgotten, and in the first paroxysm of his despair, insisted, even at the risk of falling into the hands of his former persecutors, on once more seeing Marguerite, if it were only to reproach her for infidelity; but Paul, more calm and less credulous, made him pledge his word that he would not land until he had heard from him; then, being assured that the marriage would not take place in less than fifteen days, he set out for Paris, and was received by the king, who presented him with a sword, the hilt of which was of gold, and decorated him with the order of military merit. Paul had availed himself of the kindness of the king towards him to relate to him Lusignan's adventures, and had obtained not only his pardon, but also as a reward for his late services, the appointment of Governor of Guadaloupe. All these cares had not prevented him from keeping sight of Emanuel. Being informed of the count's intended departure, he left Paris, and having written to Lusignan, appointing a place of meeting, he arrived at Auray an hour after the young count.

After their joyful meeting, Paul and Lusignan remained together until nearly twilight. Then Paul, who, as he had told Emanuel, had a personal revelation to receive, left his friend and again took the road to Auray. But this time he was on foot, and did not enter the castle, but going along the park wall, he directed his steps toward an iron gate which opened into a wood belonging to the domains of Auray.

About an hour before Paul left the fisherman's hut, where he had found Lusignan, a person had preceded him on the road toward the cottage at which he was to ask the revelation of the secret of his birth; that person was the Marchioness d'Auray, the haughty heiress of the name of Sable. She was attired in her usual mourning garments with the addition of a long black veil, which enveloped her from head to foot. Moreover, the habitation which our young adventurer, with the hesitation of ignorance, was seeking for, was to her familiar. It was a sort of keeper's house, situated at a few paces from the entrance to the park, and inhabited by an old man, in whose behalf the Marchioness d'Auray had for twenty years fulfilled one of those acts of sedulous benevolence which had gained for her in that part of Lower Brittany, the reputation of rigid holiness which she enjoyed. These attentions to age were given, it is true, with the same gloomy and solemn face which we have observed in her, and which the tender emotions of pity never softened; but they were nevertheless afforded, and all knew it, with careful punctuality.

The face of the Marchioness d'Auray was even more grave than it was wont to be, while she crossed the park to repair to the dwelling of a man who was said to be an old servant of the family. The door was standing open as if to allow the last rays of the setting sun to penetrate into the house, so sweet and balmy to old people in the month of May. The house was however empty. The Marchioness d'Auray entered it, looked around her, and then as if certain that the person she was in search of would not be long absent, she resolved to await his return. She sat down. She had remained there about half an hour, motionless and absorbed in her reflections, when she saw, between her and the declining daylight, a shadow cast before the door. She slowly raised her eyes and recognised the person she had been expecting. They both started as though they had met by chance, and were not in the habit of seeing each other every day.

"It is you, Achard," said the marchioness, who was the first to speak. "I have been waiting for you half an hour. Where can you have been?"

"Had your ladyship walked fifty paces farther, you would have found me under the large oak, on the edge of the forest."

"You know I never walk that way," said the marchioness, with a visible shudder.

"And you are wrong, madam; there is one in heaven who has a right to our joint prayers, and who, perhaps, is astonished to hear only those of old Achard."

"And how know you that I do not also pray?" said the marchioness, with a certain degree of feverish agitation. "Do you believe that the dead require we should be constantly kneeling on their tombs?"

"No," replied the old man, with a feeling of profound sorrow; "no, I do not believe that the dead are so exacting, madam; but I believe if any part of us lives under ground, it would thrill at the noise caused by the steps of those whom we have loved during our life."

"But," said the marchioness, in a low and hollow tone, "if that love were a guilty passion?"

"However guilty it may have been, madam," replied the old man, also lowering his voice, "do you not believe that blood and tears have expatiated it? God was then, believe me, too severe a judge, not to have now become an indulgent father."

"Yes, God has perhaps pardoned it," murmured the marchioness, "but did the world know that which God knows, would it pardon as God has done?"

"The world!" exclaimed the old man; "the world! Yes, there is the great word which has again escaped your lips! The world! It is to it, to that phantom you have sacrificed everything, madam; your feelings as a lover, your feelings as a wife, your feelings as a mother! your own happiness, the happiness of others! The world! It is the fear of the world which has clothed you in perpetual mourning, beneath which you hope to conceal remorse! And in that you are right, for you have succeeded in deceiving it, for it has taken your remorse for virtue!"

The marchioness raised her head with some degree of agitation, and putting aside her veil that she might look upon the person who addressed her in such extraordinary language; then, after a momentary silence, not being able to discover any sinister expression in the calm features of the old man.

"You speak to me," she said to him, "with a bitterness which would lead me to believe you have some personal reason for reproaching me. Have I failed in any promise I have made? The persons who attend on you by my orders, are they wanting in that respect which I have desired them to observe? You know, if this should be the case, you have only to say a word."

"Forgive me, madam, it is in sorrow that I speak, not bitterness; it is the effect of solitude and of age. You must well know what it is to have sorrows that you cannot speak of—tears which we dare not shed, and which fall back, drop by drop, upon the heart! No, I have not to complain of any one, madam, since first, from a feeling for which I am truly grateful, without seeking to know whence it emanated, you have been pleased to see personally that my wants were all supplied, and you have not for a single day forgotten your promise, but like the old prophet, I have sometimes seen an angel come as your messenger."

"Yes," replied the marchioness, "I know that Marguerite often accompanies the servant who is charged to wait upon you; and I have seen with pleasure the attentions she has paid you, and the friendship she feels for you."

"But in my turn, I have not failed either, I trust, in the promises I made. For twenty years I have lived far from the habitations of men, I have kept away every living being from this dwelling; so much did I fear on your account, the delirium of my waking hours, or the indiscretion of my dreams."

"Undoubtedly! undoubtedly! and happily the secret has been well preserved," said the marchioness, placing her hand upon Achard's arm; "but this is a stronger incentive in my mind not to lose in a single day the fruit of twenty years, all more gloomy, more isolated, and more terrible than yours have been."

"Yes, I understand you perfectly; and you have shuddered more than once upon suddenly remembering that there is roaming about the world, a man who may one day call upon me to reveal that secret, and that I have not the right to conceal it from that man. Ah! you tremble at the bare idea, do you not? But, tranquilise yourself; that man, when but a boy, fled from the school at which we had placed him in Scotland, and for ten years past nothing has been heard of him. In short, destined to obscurity, he himself rushed forward to meet his fate. He is now lost amid the millions that crowd this populous world, and not a soul knows where to find him; this poor unit, without a name, is lost for ever. He must have lost his father's letter, have mislaid the token by which I was to recognise him; or, better still, perhaps he exists no longer."

"It is cruel of you, Achard," replied the marchioness, "to utter such words to a mother. You cannot appreciate the strange feelings and singular contradictions contained in the heart of woman. For, in fine, can I not be tranquil unless my child be dead! Consider, my old friend; this secret, of which he has been ignorant five and twenty years, has it become at the age of twenty-five, so necessary to his existence that he cannot live, unless it be revealed to him? Believe me, Achard, for himself even it would be better he should still remain ignorant of it, as he has been to this day. I feel assured that to this day he has been happy—old man, do not mar this happiness—do not inspire his mind with thoughts which may induce him to commit an evil action. No—tell him, in lieu of the dreadful tale you were desired to communicate, that his mother has gone to rejoin his father in heaven; and, would to God that it were so! but that when dying (for I must see him whatever you may say to the contrary, I will even if it be but once, press him to my heart), when dying, as I said, his mother had bequeathed him to her friend the Marchioness d'Auray, in whom he will find a second mother."

"I understand you, madam," said Achard, smiling. "It is not the first time you have pointed out this path, in which you wish to lead me astray. Only to-day, you speak more openly, and if you dared to do so, or if you knew me less, you would offer me some reward to induce me to disobey the last injunctions of him who sleeps by us."

The marchioness made a gesture as if about to interrupt him.

"Listen to me, madam," hastily said the old man, stretching forth his hand, "and let my words be considered by you as holy and irrevocable. As faithful as I have been to the promise which I made to the Marchioness d'Auray, so faithful will I be to that I made to the Count de Morlaix, on the day when his son, or your son, shall present himself before me with the token of recognition, and shall demand to know the secret. I shall reveal it to him, madam. As to the papers which attest it, you are aware that they are to be delivered to him only after the death of the Marquis d'Auray. The secret is here," said the old man, placing his hand upon his heart; "no human power could have extracted it before the time; no human power, that time having arrived, can prevent me from revealing it. The papers are there in that closet, the key of which I always have about me, and it is only by robbery or by assassination that I can be deprived of them."

"But," said the marchioness, half rising and supporting herself on the arm of her chair, "you might die before my husband, old man; for although he is more dangerously ill than you are, you are older than he is, and then what would become of those papers?"

"The priest who shall attend my last moments will receive them under the seal of confession."

"Ah! it is that!" cried the marchioness, rising, "and thus this chain of fears will be prolonged until my death! and the last link of it will be to all eternity rivetted to my tomb. There is in this world a man, the only one perhaps, who is as immoveable as a rock; and God has placed him in my path, not only as a remorse,' but as a vengeance also. My secret is in your hands, old man,—tis well!—do with it as you will!— you are the master, and I am your slave—farewell!"

So saying, the marchioness left the cottage, and returned towards the chateau.

CHAPTER VIII.—THE SECRET.

More than ten years have passed since I beheld him,
The noble boy; now time annuls my oath
And cancels all his wrongs.
I took a solemn oath to veil the secret,
Conceal thy rights, while lived her lord,
And thus allow'd thy youth to quit my roof.

Bulwer.—*The Sea Captain.*

"Yes," said the old man, gazing after the marchioness as she withdrew, "yes, I know you have a heart of adamant, madam, insensible to every sort of fear, with the exception of that which God has placed within your breast to supply the place of remorse. But that suffices; and it is dearly buying that reputation you have obtained for virtue, to pay the price of such eternal terrors. It is true that the virtue of the Marchioness d'Auray is so firmly established, that if truth herself were to rise from the earth or to descend from heaven to arraign her, she would be treated as a calumniator. But God orders all things according to His will, and what He does ordain, His wisdom has long before matured."

"Rightly reasoned," cried a youthful and sonorous voice, replying to the religious axiom which the resignation of the old man had led him to utter. "Upon my word, good father, you speak like Ecclesiastes." Achard turned round and perceived Paul, who had arrived just as the marchioness left him, but who was so absorbed by the scene we have just

95

described, that she had not observed the young captain. The latter, seeing the old man alone, approached him, and not hearing the last words he had uttered, had spoken with his usual good humor. Achard, who was surprised by his unexpected appearance, looked at him as if he wished him to repeat that which he had said.

"I say," resumed Paul, "that there is more grandeur in resignation that humbly bows itself, than in philosophy that doubts. That is a maxim of our quakers, which, for my eternal welfare, I wish I had less often on my tongue, and more frequently in my heart."

"I beg your pardon, sir," said the old man on seeing our adventurer, who was fixedly gazing at him, while standing with one foot on the threshold of his door. "May I know who you are?"

"For the moment," replied Paul, giving, as usual, free course to his poetical and heedless gaiety, "I am a child of the republic of Plato, having all human kind for brothers, the world for a country, and possessing upon this earth only the station I have worked out for myself."

"And what are you in search of?" continued the old man, smiling in spite of himself at the air of jovial good-nature which was spread over the features of the young man.

"I am seeking," replied Paul, "at three leagues distance from Lorient, at five hundred paces from resembles this one, and in which I am to find an old man, whom it is very likely is yourself."

"And what is the name of this old man?"

"Louis Achard."

"That is my name."

"Then may the blessing of heaven descend on your white hairs," said Paul, in a voice which at once changing its tone, assumed that of deep feeling and respect; "for here is a letter which I believe was written by my father, in which he says that you are an honest man."

"Does not that letter enclose something?" cried d'Auray, and advancing a step nearer to the young captain.

"It does," replied the latter, opening the letter and taking out of it one half of a Venetian sequin, which had been broken in two; "it seems to be part of a gold coin, of which I have one half, and you ought to be in possession of the other."

Achard mechanically held out his hand, while gazing with intense interest at the young man.

"Yes, yes," said the old man, and eyes gradually became more and more suffused with tears: "yes, this is the true token, and more than that, the extraordinary resemblance," and opening his arms, he cried, "child!—oh! my God! my God!"

"What is it?" cried Paul, extending his arms to support the old man, who was quite overcome by his emotions.

"Oh! can you not comprehend?" replied the latter, "can you not comprehend that you are the living portrait of your father, and that I loved your father—loved him so much that I would have shed my blood, have given my life to serve him, as I would now for you, young man, were you to demand it."

"Embrace me, then, my old friend," said Paul, throwing

his arms around the old man, "for the chain of feeling, believe me, is not broken, which extended from the tomb of the father to the cradle of the son. Whatever my father may have been, if in order to resemble him it be only necessary to have a conscience without reproach, undaunted courage, and a memory which never forgets a benefit conferred, although it may sometimes forget an injury; if this be so, then am I, as you have said, my father's living portrait, and more so in soul than in form."

"Yes, he possessed all these," replied the old man, with solemnity, and clasping Paul to his breast, looking at him with affectionate though tearful tenderness—"Yes, he had the same commanding voice, the same flashing eyes, the same nobleness of heart. But why was it that I have not seen you sooner, young man? I have, during my life, passed many gloomy hours, which your presence would have brightened."

"Why—because this letter told me to seek you out only when I should have attained the age of twenty-five, and because it is not long since I attained that age, not more than an hour ago."

The old man bowed down his head with a pensive air, and remained silent for some time, seemingly absorbed by recollections of the past.

"Can it be so?" at length ne said, raising his head, "can it be twenty-five years ago. Good heaven! it appears to me only yesterday that you were born in this house, that you first saw the light in that very room:" and the old man raised his head, and pointed to a door which led into another room.

Paul, in his turn, appeared to reflect, and then, looking around him, to strengthen by the aid of objects which presented themselves to his view, the recollections which crowded on his memory.

"In this cottage, in that room," he repeated, "and I lived here till I was five years old, did I not?"

"Yes," murmured the old man, as if fearful to disturb the feelings which were taking possession of the young man's mind.

"Well," continued Paul, leaning his head on both his hands, as if to concentrate his thoughts, "allow me for one moment to look back, in my turn, to the past, for I am recollecting a room which I had thought I had seen in a dream—it may be that one. Listen to me! Oh! how strange it is—remembrances now rush upon me."

"Speak, my child, speak!" said the old man.

"It it be that room, there ought to be on the right, as you go in, at the end of the room, a bed with green hangings."

"Yes."

"A crucifix at the head of the bed."

"Yes."

"A closet opposite, in which were books, among the rest a large Bible, with numerous engravings."

"There it is," said the old man, pointing to the sacred book which was lying open on a desk for prayer.

"Oh! it is that—it is that," cried Paul, pressing his lips against the leaves.

"Oh! good and pious heart," cried the old man, "I thank

thee, oh! my God—I thank thee."

"Then," said Paul, rising, "in that room there is a window, from which you can discern the sea, and on the sea, three islands?"

"Yes, Houat, Hoedic, and Belle-Ileen-mer.

"Then, it is really so," said Paul, rushing towards the room, and then perceiving that the old man was about to follow him, he said: "No, no! I must be alone—let me enter it alone—I feel that I must be alone," and he went into the room, closing the door after him.

He then paused a moment, impressed with that holy respect which accompanies the remembrance of our infancy. The room was as he had described it, for the religious devotedness of the old servant had preserved it from any change. Paul, feeling doubtless that the eye of a stranger would have interrupted the expression of the feelings he experienced, and now certain of being alone, abandoned himself to them He slowly advanced, and with clasped hands, towards the ivory crucifix; and falling on his knees, which formerly he had the habit of doing, morning and evening, he endeavoured to remember one of those simple prayers, in which a child, still on the threshold of this life, prays to God for those who have opened its gates to him. "What events had succeeded each other in the lapse of time which had passed between these genuflexions! Paul remained for a considerable time absorbed in thought, and then slowly arose, and went to the window. The night was beautiful and calm, the moon was shining in the heavens, and tipped the ocean waves with silver. The three islands appeared on the horizon, like blue vapor floating on the ocean. He remembered how often in his infancy he had leaned against that window, gazing upon that same scene, following with his eyes some bark, with its snowy sails, which glided silently over the sea, like the wing of a night bird. Then his heart swelled with sweet and tender recollection; his head fell upon his chest, and silent tears ran down his cheeks. At that moment he felt that some one pressed his hands—it was the old man—he wished to conceal his emotions; but instantly repenting this vain feeling, he turned toward Achard, and frankly let him see his face, down which the tears were streaming.

"You weep, my child," said the old man.

"Yes, I weep," replied Paul; "and why should I conceal it? Yea, look at me. And yet I have, during my life, witnessed dreadful scenes. I have seen the tempest bear my vessel to the summit of a mountain wave, and then sink her into an abyss, from which I thought she would never rise again; and I felt that she weighed no more upon the wings of the storm than does a dried leaf on the evening breeze. I have seen men fall around me like the ripe ears of corn before the sickle of the reaper. I have heard the cries of distress, and the dying groans of those whose meal I had shared but the day before. In order to receive their last sigh, I have walked amid a shower of bullets, and grape-shot, upon a plank slippery with blood. And yet, amid all this, my soul was calm—my eyes remained unmoistened. But this room, see you; this room, of which I had retained so holy a remembrance; this room, in which

I had received the first caresses of a father whom I shall never see again, and the last kisses of a mother who perhaps desires no more to see me; this room is sacred as a cradle and as a tomb. I cannot thus revisit it without giving vent to my emotions; I must weep, or I shall suffocate." The old man clasped him in his arms. Paul leaned his head upon his shoulder, and during some time nothing was heard but his sobs. At length the old servant rejoined:

"Yes, you are right; this room is at once a cradle and a tomb; it was there that you were born;" he pointed to one corner with his hand; "and it was there that you received the last blessing of your father," continued he, pointing to the opposite side of the room.

"He is then dead?" said Paul.

"He is dead."

"You must tell me how he died."

"I will tell you all."

"Defer it for a moment," added Paul, as he reached a chair and seated himself, "for I am now too weak to listen to you. Let me recover myself." He placed his elbow on the window-sill, leaned his head upon his hand, and once more cast his eyes upon the sea.

"What a magnificent spectacle is the ocean when the moon shines upon it as brightly as it does now," continued he, with that accent of soft melancholy which was habitual to him. "It is as calm as God himself, and vast as eternity. I do not believe that a man accustomed to study such a scene can be afraid of death. My father met death bravely, did he not?"

"Assuredly!" proudly replied Achard.

"It could not be otherwise," continued Paul, "for I remember my father, although I was only four years old when I last saw him."

"He was a handsome young man, as you yourself are," said Achard, looking sorrowfully at Paul, "and just as old as you are."

"What was his name?"

"The Count de Moraix."

"Then I also am of an old and noble family. I also have arms and an escutcheon as well as those young and insolent nobles who ask me for my parchments when I show them my wounds?"

"Wait, young man, wait; do not allow pride to carry you thus away, for I have not yet told you the name of her who gave you being, and you are still ignorant of the dreadful secret of your birth."

"Well: be it so. I shall not with the less respect and veneration hear the name of my mother. What was my mother's name?"

"The Marchioness d'Auray," slowly replied the old man, as if regretting that he was compelled to mention her name.

"What is it that you tell me!" cried Paul, starting from his chair, and seizing the hands of the old man.

"The truth!" replied Achard, sorrowfully.

"Then Emanuel is my brother—Marguerite is my sister."

"Do you then already know them?" exclaimed the old servant, much astounded.

"Oh! you were right, old man," said Paul, throwing himself into his chair. "God orders all things according to His will, and what He does ordain, His wisdom has long before matured."

They both remained silent for a time, when at length Paul raised his head, and resolutely fixing his eyes on the old man's face, said:

"Now, I am ready to hear all you have to communicate— you may go on."

CHAPTER IX.—FATAL LOVE.

I shall a tale unfold
Will harrow up thy soul; freeze thy young blood;
Make thy two eyes like stars, start from their spheres;
Thy knotted and combined locks to part.
And each particular hair to stand on end,
Like quills upon the fretful porcupine.

Shakespeare.

The old man seemed to be summoning up his recollections for a time, and then began:

"They were affianced to each other. I know not what mortal hatred it was that arose between the families and separated them. The Count de Morlaix, broken hearted, could not remain in France. He sailed for Saint Domingo, where his father possessed a large estate; I accompanied him, for the Count de Morlaix reposed much confidence in me. I was the son of her who had nursed him; I had received the same education as himself; he used to call me his brother, and I alone remembered the distance which nature had placed between us. The Marquis de Morlaix confided to me the charge of watching over his son, for I loved him with all the love of a father. We remained two years under a tropical sun; during that two years, your father, lost amid the solitude of that magnificent island, a traveller without an object and without an aim, an ardent and indefatigable sportsman, endeavouring to cure the griefs of the mind, by the fatigues of the body; but so far from succeeding, one would have thought that his heart became still more inflamed under that ardent sun. At length, after two years of trial and incessant struggles, his love conquered. He must either see her again or die. I yielded and we set sail for France. Never was a voyage more beautiful, or more prosperous. The sea and sky seemed to smile upon us; so favourable were they that it would have induced one to believe in lucky omens. Six weeks after our departure from Port au Prince, we landed at Havre. Mademoiselle de Sablé was married. The Marquis d'Auray was at Versailles, fulfilling at the court of Louis XV. the duties of his charge, and his wife, who was too much indisposed to follow him, was at the old chateau d'Auray, the turrets of which you see from this place."

"Yes, yes," said Paul, "I know it; pray go on."

"As to myself," rejoined the old map, "during our voyage, one of my uncles, an old servant of the house of Auray, had died, and left me this small house, with a small quantity of land surrounding it. I took possession of it. Your father had left me at Vannes, telling me he was going to Paris, and for the whole of the first year that I inherited this house I did not see him."

"One night,—it is exactly twenty-five years ago,—some one knocked at my door; I went to open it and found your father there, carrying in his arms a woman whose face was veiled. He brought her into this room, and laid her on that bed. And then returning to me in the adjoining room, where I was waiting mute and motionless with astonishment, he placed his hand upon my shoulder, and looking at me in a supplicating manner, although he had the right to command me, said, 'Louis, you can do more than save my life and honor—you can save the life and honor of her I love—get on horseback, gallop to the next town, and return here in an hour with a doctor.' He spoke to me in that short and hasty tone, which indicated that there was not a moment to be lost. I immediately obeyed. The day was beginning to break when we returned. The doctor was introduced by the Count de Morlaix into this room, the door of which was immediately closed: he remained there during the whole day; towards five in the afternoon, the doctor left the house, and at nightfall your father also left the house carrying in his arms the mysterious veiled lady whom he had brought the previous night. When they had gone, I came into this room and found you here—you had just been born."

"And how did you learn that this woman was the Marchioness d'Auray?"

"Oh!" exclaimed the old man, in a way which was as terrible as it was unexpected; "I had offered the Count de Morlaix to keep you here, and he accepted my proposal: from time to time he would come to spend an hour with you."

"Alone?" demanded Paul, with much anxiety.

"Yes, always; but as he had given me permission to walk with you in the park, it would sometimes happen that at the corner of one of the avenues I would meet the marchioness, whom chance appeared to have conducted in that direction. She would make you a sign to come to her, and she would kiss you as people kiss a strange child, because he is handsome. Four years passed on in this way, and then one night some one again knocked at this door, and it was again your father. He was more calm, but had, perhaps, a more gloomy look than on the first occasion. 'Louis,' said he, 'to-morrow, at the break of day, I have to meet the Marquis d'Auray. It is a duel in which one of us must fall, and you are to be the only witness of it. The terms are agreed upon. You must, therefore, give me shelter for this night, and let me have materials for writing.' He sat down at this table, on the very chair you are now seated."

Paul sprang up, but supported himself on the back of the chair, without again sitting down upon it. "He sat up all night. At day-break he came into my room and found me up—I had not gone to bed. As to you poor child, unconscious of the passions and miseries of this life, you were quietly sleeping."

"And then,—pray go on."

"Your father bent slowly over you, supporting himself by the wall, and looking sorrowfully upon you: 'Louis,' said he to me, in a hollow voice, 'should I be killed, and which may happen, wo to this child! You will deliver him with this letter to Field, my valet de chambre, whom I have charged to conduct him to Selkirk, in Scotland, there to leave him in sure hands. When he is twenty-five years old, he will bring you the other half of this gold coin, and will ask you to reveal to him the secret of his birth. You will communicate it; for then, perhaps, his mother will be alone and isolated. As to these papers which prove his birth, you will not deliver them to him, until after the death of the Marquis d'Auray. Now I have said all that is necessary, let us go, for it is the appointed hour. He then leaned over your bed, bent down toward you, and although he was a man of fortitude, as I have told you, I saw a tear fall upon your cheek."

"Proceed," said Paul, in a voice choked by emotion.

"The rendezvous was in one of the avenues of the park, about a hundred paces from this house. When we reached the place, we found the marquis there, he had been waiting for us some minutes. Near him upon a bank were pistols ready loaded. The adversaries bowed to each other without exchanging a word. The marquis pointed to the weapons— they each took one, and then, according to the terms which had been agreed upon, as your father had told me, they placed themselves, mute and gloomily, at the distance of thirty paces, and then began to walk towards each other. Oh! it was a moment ef agony for me, I can assure you," rejoined the old man, almost as much moved as if the scene were then actually passing before him, "when I saw the distance gradually diminishing between these two men. When they were only about ten paces, the marquis stopped and fired. I looked at your father; not a muscle of his face was moved, so that I thought him safe and unhurt. He continued to walk on till he came close to the marquis, and then placing the muzzle of the pistol to his heart—"

"He did not kill him, I trust," cried Paul seizing the old man's arm.

"He said to him, Your life is in my hands, sir, and I might

take it, but I wish you to live, that you may pardon me, as I do you. And uttering these words, he fell dead at the feet of the marquis, whose ball had passed through his chest."

"Oh! my father! my father!" cried Paul, wringing his hands. "And the man who killed my father—he still lives, does he not? He is still young, and has strength enough to wield a sword or raise a pistol? We will go to him—to-day—instantly! You will tell him, that it is his son! that he must fight with him."

"God has avenged your father," replied Achard—"that man is mad."

"That is true—I had forgotten that," murmured Paul.

"And in his madness that bloody scene is ever before his eyes, and he repeats ten times a day the dying words your father addressed to him."

"And that must be the reason why the marchioness will not leave him for a single moment."

"And that is also the reason, under the pretext that he will not see his children, that she keeps Emanuel and Marguerite from him."

"My poor sister," said Paul, with an accent of undefinable tenderness; "and now she wishes to sacrifice her by forcing her to marry that wretch Lectoure."

"Yes, but that wretch Lectoure will take Marguerite with him to Paris, and give a regiment of dragoons to her brother, so that the marchioness will no longer have cause to dread the presence of her children. Her secret, therefore, remains henceforward in the breasts of two old men, who to-morrow, this night even, may die. The grave is silent."

"But, I—I!"——

"You! Does she know that you still exist! Has anything been heard of you since you escaped from Selkirk? Could not some accident have prevented you from coming to the appointment, which fortunately you have done safely? It is certain that she has not forgotten you, but she hopes"——

"Oh! can you believe that my mother"——

"I beg your pardon, that is true. I do not believe it!" cried Achard, "I was wrong; forget what I have said."

"Yes, yes, let us speak of you, my friend; let us speak of my father."

"Is it necessary that I should tell you that his last wishes were fulfilled. Field came to fetch you during the day, and took you away with him. Twenty-one years have passed since then, and since then not a single day has passed without my putting up a prayer that I might see you at the appointed time. My prayers have been granted," continued the old man; "and thanks be to God, you are here. Your father lives again in you—I once more see him—I am speaking to him. I weep no longer, I am now consoled."

"And he died thus, instantly, without a struggle, without a sigh?"

"Yes—I brought him here. I placed him on the bed in which you were born—I closed the door that no one might enter the house, and I went alone and dug his grave. I passed the whole day in this painful duty; for, according to the request of your father, to no one was to be confided this dreadful secret. In the evening I returned for the body. The heart of man is singularly constituted, and hope which God has planted in it can with difficulty be eradicated. I had seen him fall—I had felt his hands grow cold—I had kissed his ice-like face—I had left him, to hollow out his grave, and that grave being made, that duty being accomplished, I returned with a beating heart, for it appeared to me, although a miracle would be required for such a change, that during my absence life had returned to him, and that he would rise from his bed and speak to me. I entered the house—alas! alas! the days of miracles had passed away. Lazarus remained lying on his couch—dead! dead! dead!" and the old man remained for some time overwhelmed with grief, silent and voiceless, and tears rolled down his furrowed cheeks.

"Yes, yes," cried Paul, also bursting into tears; "yes, and you then fulfilled your holy mission. Good old man, let me kiss those hands which deposited my father in his last home. And you have remained faithful to his tomb as you had been to him during life. Poor guardian of the sepulchre; you have remained near him that your tears might water the grass which grew about the unknown grave. Oh! how little are those who think themselves great because their name resounds amid the tempest, and the cry of war, louder than the storm or the din of battle, in comparison with you, old man, whose devotedness has been mute and noiseless. Oh! give me your blessings lay those hallowed hands upon my head, since my father is not here to bless me," continued Paul, throwing himself on his knees before him.

"Rise to my arms—let me clasp you to my heart, my child, for you exaggerate these actions, in themselves so simple and so natural. And then, believe me, that which you term my piety has not been a useless lesson to me. I have seen how little space a man occupies beneath the ground, and how soon he is lost amid the world, should God turn his face from him. Your father was young, full of courage, with a brilliant career opening before him. Your father was the last descendant of an ancient line; he bore a noble name. His path seemed marked with honors and distinction; he had a family and powerful friends. Well, he suddenly disappeared, as if the earth had opened beneath his feet. I know not if some tearful eyes sought for him till they lost all trace of him; but this I know, that for one-and-twenty years no one has sought out his tomb—no one knows that he lies beneath that spot, where the grass is greener and grows more luxuriantly than elsewhere—and yet, vain, glorious, and miserable as he is, man considers himself of some value."

"Oh! and my mother, has she not visited his grave?"

The old man did not answer.

"Well, then! there will be two of us who henceforward will know the spot, where he reposes. Come, and show it to me; for I will return to it, I promise solemnly, every time my ship returns to the coast of France."

Saying this, he drew Achard into the outer room, but as they opened the door they heard a slight noise in the park. It was a servant from the castle, who had accompanied Marguerite. Paul hurriedly returned into the bedroom.

"It is my sister," said he to Achard; "leave me alone with her a moment. It is necessary that I should speak to her. I have something to communicate which will make her pass a happy night. We must have compassion for those who watch and weep."

"Reflect," said Achard, "that the secret I have revealed to you is your mother's."

"Fear not—I will speak to her but of that which concerns herself."

At that moment Marguerite entered the room.

CHAPTER X.—CONFIDENCE.

This ring I gave him when he parted from me
To bind him to remember my good will;
The more shame for him that he sends it to me.

Shakespeare.

Marguerite had come, as she frequently did, to bring some provisions for the old man, and it was not without astonishment that she perceived in the outer room, where she usually found Achard, a young and handsome man, who looked at her with gladdened eyes, and with a kindly smile. She made a sign to the servant to put down the basket in a corner of the room; he obeyed, and then went out to wait for his mistress in the park. When he had withdrawn, she advanced towards Paul, saying,—

"I beg your pardon, sir, but I expected to find my old friend, Achard, here, and I came, to bring him something from my mother"—

Paul pointed to the inner room, to let her know that the person she was seeking was within, for he could not reply to her; he felt that the tone of his voice would betray the emotions he experienced. The young girl thanked him, with a bow, and went into the room to find Achard.

Paul followed her with his eyes—his hand pressed upon his heart. That virgin soul into which love had never penetrated, now expanded with fraternal tenderness. Isolated as he had always been, having no friends but the rude

115

children of the ocean, all that was soft or tender in his heart, he had turned towards God, and although in the eyes of rigid Christians, his religion might not have appeared as strictly orthodox, it is no less true, that the poetry which overflowed in every word he uttered was nothing more than one vast and eternal prayer. It was not, therefore, astonishing, that this first feeling which penetrated his heart, although purely fraternal, was as extravagant and transporting as the emotions of love.

"Oh!" murmured he, "poor isolated being that I am! How shall I be able to restrain my feelings when she returns, and prevent myself from clasping her to my heart and saying to her: Marguerite! my sister, no woman has yet felt love for me; love me then with sisterly affection. Oh! mother! mother! by depriving me of your caresses, you have also deprived me of those of this dear angel. May God restore to you in eternity that happiness which you have driven from yourself and others."

"Farewell!" said Marguerite to the old man, opening the door, "farewell! I wished this evening to come myself, for I know not when I may see you again."

And she went toward the outer door, pensive, and with her eyes cast down, without seeing Paul, without remembering that a stranger was in that room. Paul remained gazing at her with outstretched arms as if to prevent her leaving the house, with palpitating heart and moistened eyes. At length, when he saw her placing her hand upon the door-latch, he cried aloud—

"Marguerite!"

She turned round amazed, but not being able to comprehend this strange familiarity, in one who was totally unknown to her, she half-opened the door.

"Marguerite!" reiterated Paul, advancing a step towards his sister, "Marguerite, do you not hear me call you?"

"It is true that my name is Marguerite, sir," she replied, with dignity; "but I could not imagine that word was addressed to me by a person whom I have the honor of knowing."

"But I know you!" exclaimed Paul, going nearer to her, and then closing the door he brought her back into the room. "I know that you are unhappy, that you have not one friendly heart into which you can pour your sorrows, not one arm from which you can ask support."

"You forget the one which is on high," replied Marguerite, raising her eyes and hand toward heaven.

"No, no, Marguerite, I do not forget, for it is He who sends me to offer you that which you most need; to tell you when all lips and all hearts are closed toward you, 'I am your friend, devotedly, eternally.'"

"Oh! sir!" replied Marguerite, "these are sacred and solemn words which you have uttered; words, unfortunately, to which it would be difficult for me to give credence without proofs."

"And should I give you one?" said Paul.

"Impossible!" murmured Marguerite.

"Irrefragable!" continued Paul.

"Oh! then!" exclaimed Marguerite, with an indescribable

accent, in which doubt began to give place to hope—

"Well! and then"—

"Oh! then—but no, no!"

"Do you know this ring?" said Paul, showing her the one with the key that opened the bracelet.

"Gracious heaven!" exclaimed Marguerite, "have mercy upon me! he is dead!"

"He lives."

"Then he no longer loves me."

"He loves you!"

"If he be living—if he still love me—oh! I shall go mad—what was it I was saying? If he be living—if he still love me, how comes it that this ring is in your possession?"

"He confided it to me as a token of recognition."

"And have I confided this bracelet to any one?" cried Marguerite, pushing back the sleeve of her gown—"Look!"

"Yes, but you, Marguerite, you are not proscribed—dishonored, in the eyes of the whole world—thrown amongst a condemned race!"

"Of what importance is that. Is he not innocent?"

"And then, he thought," continued Paul, wishing to discover the extent of the devotedness and love of his sister, "he thought that delicacy required, banished as he is for ever from society, that he should offer you, if not restore to you, the liberty of disposing of your hand."

"When a woman has done for a man that which I have done for him," replied Marguerite, "her only excuse is to love him eternally, and it is that I mean to do."

"Oh! you are an angel!" exclaimed Paul.

"Tell me!" rejoined Marguerite, seizing the young man's hands, and looking at him with a supplicating air—

"What?"

"Have you seen him, then?"

"I am his friend, his brother."

"Speak to me of him, then?" she exclaimed, giving herself up entirely to the recollection of her lover, and forgetting that it was the first time she had seen the person to whom she was addressing questions of so delicate a nature. "What is he doing? what hope has he? Poor, unhappy man!"

"He loves you—and he hopes again to see you."

"Then, then," stammered Marguerite, and drawing back some paces,—"he has told you——?"

"All!"

"Oh!" she cried, looking down and concealing her face, over which a sudden tinge of red had cast itself, replacing for a moment its habitual paleness.

Paul approached her and clasping her to his breast, exclaiming—

"You are a miracle of devotedness!"

"You do not then despise me, sir?" said Marguerite, Venturing to raise her eyes.

"Marguerite!" cried Paul, "had I a sister I would pray to heaven that she might resemble you."

"Oh! were it so you would have a most unhappy sister," she replied, leaning upon his arm and bursting into tears.

"Perhaps," said Paul, smiling.

"You know not, then——?"

"Proceed."

"That Monsieur de Lectoure is to arrive to-morrow morning."

"I have been informed of that."

"And that to-morrow night the marriage contract is to be signed."

"I know that, too."

"Well! then! what can I hope for in such extremity as this? To whom can I apply to prevent this hated union? Who can I interest to aid me? My brother? God knows that I forgive him, but he cannot comprehend my feelings. My mother? Oh! sir, you do not know my mother. She is a woman whose reputation is unsullied, of the most austere virtue, and her will inflexible, for never having failed in her duty, she does not believe that others can forget it, and when she has once said, 'It is my will,' all that remains to do is to bow down one's head, to weep, and to obey. My father? Yes, I well know that my father must leave the room from which he has never stirred for twenty years, to sign this contract. My father! for any one less unhappy and less culpable than I might prove a resource: but you know not that he is insane—that he has lost his reason, and with it every feeling of paternal affection. And besides, it is ten years since I last saw him. For the last ten years I have not pressed his trembling hands, nor kissed his snow white hairs. He knows not that he has still a daughter! he knows not even whether he has a heart, and will not be able even to recognize me. And were he but to know me, and took compassion on me, my mother would place a pen in his hand and would say, 'Sign that, it is my will!' and he would sign it—the poor feeble old man! and his daughter would be condemned."

"Yes, yes. I know all this as well as you do, my poor child; but be pacified, that contract never will be signed."

"And who can prevent it?"

"I will!"

"You?"

"Do not despair. To-morrow I shall be present at the family council."

"Who will present you there?"

"I have the means."

"My brother is violent; and passionate. Oh! good heaven, beware, while striving to save me that you do not sink me still deeper in misery?"

"Your brother's person is in my eyes as sacred as your own, Marguerite. Fear nothing, and rely confidently upon me."

"Oh! I believe you, sir, and I implicitly confide in you," said Marguerite, as if overwhelmed by the contending feelings of confidence and mistrust which she had till then labored under. "For what advantage could you derive from endeavoring to deceive me? What interest could you have to betray me?"

"None, undoubtedly; but let us talk of other matters. What line of conduct do you intend to pursue with regard to the Baron de Lectoure?"

"I will tell him all!"

"Oh!" cried Paul, bowing profoundly, "allow me to adore you."

"Sir!" murmured Marguerite, "sir!"

"As a sister! as a sister!"

"Yes, you are indeed kind and good," cried Marguerite, "and I believe it is God who sent you to my aid."

"Believe it," replied Paul. "Then—to-morrow evening."

"Do not be astonished, nor alarmed at anything that may occur, only contrive to let me know by letter, by a word, a sign, the result of your interview with Lectoure!"

"I will endeavor to do so."

"It is now late, and your servant may be surprised at the length of this interview. Return to the castle, and say not a word of me to any one. Farewell!"

"Farewell," reiterated Marguerite; "you to whom I know not what name to give."

"Call me your brother."

"Farewell, then, brother."

"Oh, my sister! my sister!" cried Paul, clasping her convulsively in his arms, "your lips are the first from which I have heard so sweet a word. God will reward you for it."

The young girl drew back amazed; and then returning to Paul, she held out her hand to him. Paul again pressed it, and Marguerite left the cottage.

The young man then went to the door of the inner room, and opened it.

"And now, good old man," said he, "conduct me to my

father's grave."

CHAPTER XI.—THE COURTIER.

Hamlet.—Dost thou know this water-fly?

Horatio.—No, my good lord.
Hamlet.—Thy state is the more gracious; for 'tis a vice to know him.

Shakespeare.

Here on my knees by heaven's blest nower I swear,
If you persist, I ne'er henceforth will see you;
But rather wander through the world a beggar,
And live on sordid scraps at poor men's doors.
For, though to fortune lost, I'll still inherit
My mother's virtues and my father's honor.

—Otway.

The day following that on which Paul had been made acquainted with the secret of his birth, the inhabitants of the castle of Auray awoke more than ever absorbed in the fears and hopes which their several interests had created, for that day must necessarily prove a decisive one to the whole of them. The marchioness, whom our readers have ere this discovered, was neither perverse or wicked, but a haughty and inflexible woman, saw in it the termination of those heart-rending apprehensions, which for so many years, had been her daily companions; for it was above all, in the eyes

124

of her children, that she wished to preserve that unsullied reputation, the usurpation of which had been purchased at such cost. To her, Lectoure was not only a fitting son-in-law, being the bearer of a name as noble as her own, but more than this, a man, or rather a good genius, who at the same moment would bear away not only her daughter, whom he would take with him as his wife, but her son also, to whom the minister, thanks to this alliance, had promised to give a regiment. Both her children gone, her first-born might come, and the secret revealed to him, would find no echo. Moreover, there were a thousand methods by which to close his lips. The fortune of the marchioness was immense, and gold was one of those resources, which, in such a case, she deemed infallible. The more terrible her fears, the more ardently did she desire this union; so that she not only encouraged the anxiety of Lectoure, but she also excited that of Emanuel. As to the latter, tired of living unknown at Paris, or immured in Brittany, lost in the crowd of brilliant young men who formed the household of the King, or shut up in the antique castle of his ancestors, having their portraits as his sole companions, he knocked with impatient eagerness at the golden door which his intended brother-in-law was to open for him, at Versailles. The grief and tears of his sister had, certainly, for a time afflicted him; for he was ambitious, more from a dread of the ennui, which would consume him if compelled to live on his estate, and from the desire of parading at the head of his regiment, captivating the hearts of all the ladies by the richness and good taste of his uniform, than from either pride or hardness of heart. Being himself incapable of forming any serious attachment, and despite the fatal consequences of his sister's love, he considered that love, merely as a childish fancy, which the tumult and pleasure of the world would soon efface from her memory, and he really believed that before a year had elapsed, she would be the first to thank him for having thus done violence to her feelings.

As to Marguerite, poor victim, so irrevocably condemned to be immolated to the fear of the one, and to the ambition of the other, the scene of the preceding day had made a profound impression on her mind. She could not at all account to herself for the extraordinary feelings which the young man who had transmitted to her the words of Lusignan, had awakened in her heart; who had tranquillized her as to the fate of the unhappy exile, and had concluded by pressing her to his heart, and calling her his sister. A vague and instinctive hope whispered to her heart, that this man, as he had told her, had received from heaven the mission to protect her. But as she was ignorant of the tie which bound him to her, of the secret which made him master of his mother's will, of the influence he might exercise over her future life, she did not dare allow herself to dream of happiness, habituated as she had been for six months, to consider death as the only term to her misfortunes.

The marquis, alone, amid the various emotions which agitated all around him, had remained coldly and impassibly indifferent; for to him the world had ceased to move since the dreadful day on which reason had abandoned him;

continually absorbed by one fixed idea, that of his mortal combat, without seconds. The only words he ever uttered, were those pronounced by the Count de Morlaix, when he forgave him his death. He was an old man, weak as an infant, and whom his wife could overawe by a gesture, and who received from her cold and continuous will, every impulsion, which, for twenty years, the vegetating instinct had received, and which, on him, had usurped the place of reason and free will. On this day, however, a great change had taken place in his monotonous mode of life. A valet de chambre had entered his apartment, and had succeeded to the marchioness in the cares of his toilette; he had dressed him in his uniform of steward of the household, had decorated his breast with the several orders that had been conferred upon him; and then the marchioness, placing a pen in his hand, had ordered him to try to sign his name, and he had obeyed, passively and negligently, without imagining that he was studying the part of an executioner.

About three in the afternoon, a postchaise, the sound of whose wheels had very differently impressed the hearts of the three persons who were expecting it, entered the court-yard of the castle. Emanuel had eagerly run down to the vestibule to receive his future brother-in-law, for it was he who had arrived. Lectoure sprang lightly from his carriage. He had halted for some time at the last post-house, to attire himself in a presentable costume, so that he arrived in an elegant court dress of the latest fashion. Emanuel smiled at this evidence of his anxiety, for it was clearly to be perceived, that Lectoure was determined not to lose the advantage of a first favorable impression, by presenting himself in a dusty travelling dress. His intercourse with the fair sex had taught him, that they almost invariably judge from the first glance, and the effect which it produces upon their minds or hearts, let it be favorable or unfavorable, is with difficulty removed. Moreover, it is but rendering justice to the baron to acknowledge that his person was graceful and elegant, and might have been dangerous to any woman whose heart was not already occupied by another.

"Permit me, my dear baron," said Emanuel, advancing toward him, "in the momentary absence of the ladies, to do the honors of the mansion of my ancestors. See," continued he, when they had reached the top of the stone steps leading into the hall, and pointing to the turrets and the bastions, "these date from the time of Philip Augustus, as to architecture, and from Henry IV., in point of ornament."

"Upon my honor," replied the baron, in the affected tone which the young men of that day had adopted, "it is a most charming fortress, and throws around it, to a distance of at least three leagues, a baronial odour, which would perfume even an army contractor. If ever," continued he, as they passed through the hall and entered a gallery ornamented on each side with long lines of family portraits, "I should take a fancy to enter into a rebellion against his most Christian Majesty, I shall entreat you to lend me this jewel of a place; and," added he, casting his eyes on the long rows of ancestors which offered themselves to his view, "the garrison with it."

"Thirty-three quarters—I will not say in flesh and blood," replied Emanuel, "for they are long since turned to dust—but in painting, as you see. They begin with a certain Chevalier Hugues d'Auray, who accompanied King Louis VII. to the crusades; that one, it is pretended, is my aunt Deborah, whom you see decked out as Judith; and all this eventually ends in the male line, in the last member of this illustrious family, your very humble and very obedient servant, Emanuel d'Auray."

"It is perfectly respectable, and nothing can be more authentic."

"Yes; but as I do not feel that I have, as yet, become sufficiently a patriarch," rejoined Emanuel, passing before the baron to show him the way to the apartment which had been prepared for him, "to spend my days in such formidable society, I hope, baron, that you have thought of the means by which I can withdraw from it?"

"Undoubtedly, my dear count," said Lectoure, following him. "I wished even to have been myself the bearer of your commission, as my wedding gift to you. I knew of a vacancy in the queen's dragoon's, and called yesterday on M. de Maurepas to solicit it for you, when I heard that it had been granted, at the request of I know not what mysterious admiral, a sort of corsair, pirate, or fantastic being, whom the queen has made the fashion by giving him her hand to kiss, and whom the king has taken a great affection to because he beat the English, I know not where—so that his majesty has conferred upon him the order of military merit, and presented him a sword with a gold hilt, just as he would have done to one of the nobility. In short, the game is lost on that side, but do not be alarmed, we will turn round to another."

"Very well," replied Emanuel, "I care not what regiment it may be in; what I desire is, that it should be a rank suitable to my name, and a position which would be becoming to our wealth."

"Precisely—you shall have them."

"But how," said Emanuel, wishing to change the subject of conversation, "how did you manage to get rid of the thousand engagements you must have had on your hands."

"Why," said the baron, with that perfectly free and easy air, which belonged only to that distinguished class, and stretching himself upon a couch, for they had at length reached the apartment destined for him, "why, by frankly stating the fact to them. I announced at the queen's card table, I was going to be married."

"Oh! good heaven! Why, this was perfect heroism! Above all, if you acknowledged you were about to seek a wife in the depths of Lower Brittany."

"I did acknowledge it."

"And then," said Emanuel, smiling, "compassion stifled every angry feeling."

"Gad! you will readily comprehend, my dear count," said Lectoure, putting one knee over the other and, balancing his leg with a motion as regular as that of a pendulum, "our women of the court believe that the sun rises at Paris, and sets at Versailles—all the rest of France, is, in their idea, a

Lapland, Greenland, Nova Zembla! So that they expect, as you have hinted, my dear count, to see me bring back with me from my voyage to the pole some large hands, and formidable feet! Fortunately, they are mistaken," he added, with an accent half timorous, half interrogatory; "is it not so, Emanuel? for you told me that your sister"——

"You will see her," replied Emanuel.

"It will be a dreadful disappointment to that poor Madame de Chaulne—it cannot be helped—and she must console herself. What is it?"

This question was induced by the entrance of Emanuel's valet-de-chambre; who had half opened the door, and remained upon the threshold, waiting, as was then the custom of all servants in great houses, till his master should address him.

"What is it? repeated Emanuel.

"Mademoiselle Marguerite d' Auray requests that Monsieur, the Baron de Lectoure, will honor her with a private interview."

"Me!" said Lectoure, rising from the sofa, "certainly, with the greatest pleasure."

"But no! it is a mistake!" exclaimed Emanuel; "you must be mistaken, Celestin."

"I have the honor to assure your lordship," replied the valet de chambre, "that I have correctly and faithfully executed the order which was given to me."

"Impossible!" said Emanuel, uneasy to the highest degree, at the step his sister had ventured to take: "Baron, if you will be advised by me, you will send the little simpleton about her business."

"By no means! by no means," replied Lectoure. "What does this bluebeard of a brother mean? Celestin! Did you not call this lad, Celestin?"

Emanuel impatiently bowed his head in the affirmative. "Well then, Celestin, tell my lovely betrothed that I throw myself at her knees, at her feet, and that I await her orders either to go to her or to receive her here;—and there, take this for the charges of your embassy."

He threw him his purse.

"And you, count," rejoined Lectoure, "I trust that you have confidence enough in me, to permit this tête-à-tête?"

"But it is so perfectly absurd!"

"Not at all," replied Lectoure; "on the contrary, it is perfectly befitting. I am not a crowned head, that I should marry a woman upon her portrait, and by proxy. I wish to see her in person. Come, Emanuel," he continued, pushing his friend toward a side door, that he might not meet his sister—"Come, now, tell me frankly—in confidence, between ourselves—is there any—deformity?"

"Why, no, by heaven!" replied the young count, "no—on the contrary, she is as lovely as an angel."

"Well, then!" said the baron, "what does all this opposition mean? Come, now, begone, or must I call my guards?"

"No; but on my word, I am afraid that this little simpleton, who has not the slightest notion of the world, is coming to destroy all that has been arranged between us."

"Oh! if that is all you fear," replied Lectoure, opening the door, "you may be perfectly at ease. I like the brother too well not to look over some caprice—some extraordinary fantasies in the sister—and I pledge you my word as a gentleman, unless the devil should play us some strange trick, (whom, I trust, is at this moment fully occupied in some other corner of the world!) that Mademoiselle Marguerite d'Auray, shall be Madame the Baroness de Lectoure, and that in a month you shall have your regiment."

This promise appeared in some degree to pacify Emanuel, who allowed himself to be pushed out of the door without making further difficulty. Lectoure immediately ran to a looking-glass to repair the slight traces of disorder, which the jolting over the three last leagues had occasioned in his dress. He had scarcely given to his, hair and garments the most becoming turn and folds, when the door again opened, and Celestin announced—

"Mademoiselle Marguerite d'Auray."

The baron turned round, and perceived his betrothed standing pale and trembling on the threshold of the door. Although the promises of Emanuel had inspired him with some degree of hope, a certain residue of doubt had still remained on his mind, if not as to the beauty, at all events, with regard to the deportment of the lady who was about to become his wife. His surprise was therefore unbounded, when he saw that delicate and graceful creature standing before him, and whom the most fastidious critic of female elegance could only have reproached with being in a slight degree too pallid. Marriages, such as the one about to be contracted by Lectoure, were by no means rare in an age in which questions as to rank and suitableness of fortune in general, decided alliances between noble houses; but that which was scarcely found once in a thousand times, was, that a man in the baron's position should meet, immured in a distant province, a lady possessed of an immense fortune, and whom, at the first glance, he could discern, was worthy, by her demeanor, her elegance, and her beauty, to shine in the most brilliant circles of the court. He, therefore, advanced toward her, no longer with the feeling of superiority as a courtier, addressing a country girl, but with all the respectful ease which distinguished good society at that time.

"Pardon me, mademoiselle," said he, offering her his hand to conduct her to an arm chair, but which she did not accept; "it was to me to solicit the favor you have bestowed upon me; and believe me, it was the apprehension of being considered indiscreet, which alone has occasioned the apparent neglect of allowing myself to be forestalled."

"I truly appreciate this delicacy, sir," replied Marguerite, in a trembling voice, and retreating one step, she remained standing. "It strengthens me still more in the confidence which, without having seen you, without knowing you, I had placed in your honor and good faith."

"Whatever aim this confidence may have had, I am honored by it, mademoiselle, and I will endeavor to render myself worthy of it. But, good heaven, what can so affect you?"

"Nothing, sir, nothing," replied Marguerite, endeavoring to overcome her emotion; "but it is—it is—that I have to tell you that—but—really—I am not sufficiently mistress of myself to—"

She staggered, and appeared as if about to fall; the baron sprang toward her to offer his support, but he had scarcely touched her when a flush of crimson suffused the cheeks of the young girl, and with a feeling, which might be attributed as well to modesty as to repugnance, she disengaged herself from his arms. Lectoure had taken her hand, and conducted her to a chair, against which she leaned, but would not seat herself in it.

"Good God!" exclaimed the baron, still retaining her hand, "it must then be something very difficult to utter, that has brought you hither! Or, without my at all suspecting it, has my being affianced to you already conferred upon me the imposing air of a husband?" Marguerite made another effort to withdraw her hand from the baron, and which induced the latter to observe it.

"How!" said he, "not satisfied with having the most adorable of faces, the elegant figure of a fairy, but you must have such lovely hands!—hands perfectly royal in their shape—why, 'tis enough to make me expire at once."

"I trust M. le Baron," rejoined Marguerite, and making a last effort, she withdrew her hand from his grasp, "that the words with which you are now addressing me, are merely words of gallantry."

"No, by my soul! they are the sincere truth."

"Well then, I hope, should it be, which I much doubt, that you really think that which you have been pleased to say—I trust, I say, that such motives will not lead you to attach a higher value to the union which has been projected?"

"They will, indeed, and that I swear to you."

"And yet," continued Marguerite, gasping for breath, so much was her heart oppressed, "and yet, sir, you consider marriage as a solemn matter?"

"That is as it may happen," smilingly replied Lectoure; "for example, if I were about to marry an old dowager."

"In short," rejoined Marguerite, in a more determined tone, "I beg your pardon, sir, if I have been mistaken; I thought, perhaps, that with regard to the alliance proposed between us, you had formed some idea of reciprocity of feeling."

"Never!" cried Lectoure, interrupting her, for he appeared as eager to avoid the frank explanation, which Marguerite desired, as she seemed to provoke it. "Never! and above all, since I have seen you, I could not hope to be worthy of your love. And yet my name, my position in society, notwithstanding I should fail to influence your heart, may yet give me a title to your hand."

"But how, sir," said Marguerite, timidly, "how can you separate the one from the other?"

"As do three-fourths of the people who get married, mademoiselle," replied Lectoure, with a carelessness which would have at once deterred the confidence of a woman less candid than Marguerite. "A man marries in order to have a wife, the wife to have a husband; it is a social compact, an arrangement of convenience. What can love have to do in a matter of this nature?"

"Your pardon, sir; perhaps I have not clearly expressed my meaning," continued Marguerite, making an effort to control her feelings, and to conceal from the man upon whom her future fate depended, the impression his words had produced upon her mind. "But you must attribute my hesitation, sir, to the timidity of a young girl, compelled by imperious circumstances to speak on such a subject."

"Not at all, mademoiselle," replied Lectoure, bowing and giving to his voice a tone which nearly approached raillery; "on the contrary, you speak like Clarissa Harlowe, and all you say is as clear as daylight. God has endowed me with a mind sufficiently quick-sighted perfectly to comprehend things which are but hinted at."

"How, sir!" cried Marguerite, "you comprehend what I had the intention of saying, and you allow me to continue? How would it be if on looking deeply into my heart and interrogating all its feelings, I found it impossible to love—to love the person who had been presented to me as my future husband?"

"Why," replied Lectoure, in the same sarcastic tone in which he had before spoken, "in my opinion the best course to pursue would be not to tell him of it."

"And why not, sir?"

"Because—but—but—because it would really be too simple."

"And if that avowal were made, not from simplicity but from delicacy? If I added, and may the shame of such an avowal fall back on those who compel me to make it—if I added sir, that I have loved, that I still love?"

"Oh! some little romance, is it not so?" said Lectoure, carelessly, crossing his leg and playing with the frill of his shirt; "upon my honor, the race of little cousins is an accursed race. But fortunately we know what these ephemeral attachments are; and there is not a school-girl, who, after the holidays, does not return to her convent but with a passion in her little heart."

"Unfortunately for me," replied Marguerite, with, a voice as sorrowful and grave as that of the baron was sarcastic and light, "unfortunately, I am no longer a school-girl, sir; and although still young, I have long ago passed the age of childish games and infantine attachments. When I speak to the man who does me the honor to solicit my hand and to offer me his name, of my love for another, he ought to understand that I am speaking of a serious, profound, and eternal love; of one of those passions, in fine, which leave their traces in the heart, and imprint them there for ever."

"The devil!" exclaimed Lectoure, as if beginning to attach some importance to Marguerite's confession; "why, this is perfectly pastoral. But let us see! is it a young man whom one can receive at one's house?"

"Oh! sir," cried Marguerite, catching at the hope which these words seemed to inspire: "oh! believe me, he is the most estimable being, the most devoted soul——"

"Why, I am not asking you to tell me this—I was not speaking of the qualities of his heart—he has all these, of course, that's perfectly understood. I ask you whether he is noble? if he is of good race? in short, whether a woman of quality could acknowledge him, and that without degrading her husband?"

"His father, whom he lost when very young, and who was my father's friend from infancy, was a counsellor at the Court of Rennes."

"Nobility of the bar!" exclaimed Lectoure, dropping his nether lip with a contemptuous shrug; "I would rather it were otherwise—is he a knight of Malta, at least?"

"He was educated for a military life."

"Oh! then, we must get a regiment for him, to give him rank and standing in society. Well, that's all arranged, and it is well. Now, listen to me: he will absent himself for six months, merely for decency's sake, will obtain leave of absence, no difficult matter now, as we are not at war—he will get himself presented to you for form's sake, by some mutual friend, and then all will go on rightly."

"I do not understand you, sir," replied Marguerite, looking at the baron with an expression of profound astonishment.

"What I have said to you is, notwithstanding, perfectly pellucid," rejoined the latter, with some show of impatience; "you have engagements on your side—I have on mine—but that is no reason for preventing an union which is perfectly suitable in every respect; and once accomplished, why, I think, we are bound to render it as bearable as we can. Do you comprehend me now?"

"Oh! pardon me, sir, pardon me," cried Marguerite, starting back, as though these words had outraged her; "I have been very imprudent, very culpable perhaps; but whatever I may have been, I did not dream I could have merited so gross an insult. Oh! sir, the blush of shame is now scorching my cheek, but more for you than for myself. Yes, I understand you—an apparent love and a concealed one; the face of vice and the mask of virtue; and it is to me—to me, the daughter of the Marquis d'Auray, that so shameful, so humiliating, so infamous a bargain is proposed. Oh!" continued she, falling into an arm-chair, and hiding her face with both her hands, "I must then be a most unfortunate, most contemptible lost creature! Oh! my God! my God!"

"Emanuel! Emanuel!" cried the baron, opening the door, at which he rightly suspected Marguerite's brother had remained; "come in, my dear friend; your sister is attacked with spasms; these things ought to be attended to, or they may become chronic; Madame do Moulan died of them. Here, take my scent bottle, and let her smell at it. As to myself, I am going down into the park. If you have nothing else to do, you can rejoin me there, and bring me, if you please, news of your sister."

Saying these words, the Baron de Lectoure left the room with miraculous calmness, leaving Marguerite and Emanuel together.

Captain Paul

CHAPTER XII.—THE CHALLENGE.

Do as you will, heap wrongs on wrongs upon me,
It shall not anger me—I tell thee Claudius,
Thou art enshrined in a holy circle
My foot can never pass—nor taunt, nor insult
Can e'er induce this hand to rise against thee.
Therefore be satisfied—
Once more I tell theo I will not fight with thee.
—*Old Play.*

On the day on which the interview between Marguerite and the Baron de Lectoure had taken place, the result of which had proved so diametrically opposed to the hopes and expectations of the young girl, on that day at four o'clock, the dinner bell recalled the baron to the castle. Emanuel did the honors of the table, for the marchioness could not leave her husband, and Marguerite had requested permission not to come down stairs. The other guests were the notary, the relations of the family, and the witnesses. The repast was a gloomy one, notwithstanding the imperturbable gaiety of Lectoure; but it was evident that by his joyous humor, so stirring that it appeared feverish, he strove to stun his own feelings. From time to time, indeed, his boisterous liveliness failed all at once, like a lamp, the oil of which is nearly extinguished, and then it suddenly burst forth again, as doth the flame when it devours its last aliment. At seven o'clock they rose from table, and went into the drawing-room. It would be difficult to form an idea of the strange aspect which the old castle then presented; the vast apartments of which were hung with damask draperies, with gothic designs, and ornamented with furniture of the times of Louis XIII. and Louis XIV.

They had been so long closed that they appeared unaccustomed to the presence of living beings. And, therefore, notwithstanding the abundance of chandeliers with which the servants had decorated the rooms, the feeble and vascillating light of the wax candles was insufficient to illuminate the vast rooms, and in which the voice resounded as under the arches of a cathedral. The small number of the guests, who were to be joined during the evening by some three or four gentlemen of the neighbourhood, increased the gloom which appeared to hover over the emblazoned columns of the castle. In the centre of one of the saloons, the same one in which Emanuel, at the moment after his arrival from Paris, had received Captain Paul, was placed a table prepared with much solemnity, on which was laid a closed portfolio, which, to the eyes of a stranger ignorant of all that was preparing, might as well have enclosed a death warrant as a marriage contract. In the midst of these grave aspects and gloomy impressions, from time to time a shrill mocking laugh would reach the ears of a group of persons whispering to each other. It proceeded from Lectoure, who was amusing himself at the expense of some good country gentlemen, without any respect for the feelings of Emanuel, upon whom a portion of his raillery necessarily recoiled. He would, however, every now and then cast an anxious glance around the room, and then a gloomy cloud would pervade his features, for he saw not either his father-in-law, or the marchioness, or Marguerite enter the room. As we have already stated, that neither of them had been present at the dinner table, and his interview with the latter had not, however careless he endeavored to appear, left him without some uneasiness with regard to the signing of the contract, which was to take place during the evening. Neither was Emanuel exempt from all anxiety, and he had just determined to go up to his sister's apartment, when in passing through one of the rooms he saw Lectoure, who made a sign to him to draw near.

"By heaven! you have come in the nick of time, my dear count," said he to him, while appearing to pay the greatest attention to a good country gentleman, who was talking to him, and of whom he seemed on terms of perfect intimacy; "here is M. de Nozay, who is relating to me some very curious things, upon my word! But do you know," continued he, turning to the narrator, "this is most admirable, and highly interesting. I also have marshes and ponds, and I must ask my steward as soon as I get to Paris, to tell me where they are situated. And do you catch many wild ducks in this way."

"An immense quantity," replied the gentleman, and with the accent of perfect simplicity, which proved that Lectoure could, without fear of detection, for some time longer sustain the conversation in the same tone.

"What, then, is this miraculous mode of sporting?"

inquired Emanuel.

"Only imagine, my dear friend," replied Lectoure, with the most complete sang froid, "that this gentleman gets into the water up to his neck,—At what time of the year, may I ask, without being indiscreet?"

"In the month of December and January."

"It is impossible that any thing can be more picturesque. I was saying, then, that he gets into the water up to his neck, puts a large toadstool over his head, and conceals himself among the bulrushes. This so completely metamorphoses him that the ducks do not recognise him, and allow him to come close to them. Did you not say so?"

"As near as I am to you."

"Bah! really?" exclaimed Emanuel.

"And this gentleman kills just as many as he pleases."

"I kill them by dozens," said he, proudly, being enchanted by the attention which the two young men were paying to the recital of his exploits.

"It must be a delightful thing for your good lady, if she be fond of ducks," said Emanuel.

"She adores them," said M. de Nozay.

"I hope you will do me the honor to introduce me to so interesting a person," said Lectoure, bowing.

"Undoubtedly baron."

"I swear to you," said Lectoure, "that instantly on my return to Paris, I will speak of this sport in the king's dressing-room, and I am persuaded that his majesty himself will make a trial of it in one of his large ponds of Versailles."

"I beg your pardon, dear marquis," said Emanuel, taking Lectoure's arm, and whispering in his ear, "this is one of our country neighbors, whom we could not do otherwise than invite on so solemn an occasion."

"It requires no apology, my dear friend," said Lectoure, using the same precaution not to be heard by the party in question: "you would have been decidedly wrong had you deprived me of so amusing a companion. He is an appendage to the dower of my future wife, and I should have been greatly chagrined not to have made his acquaintance."

"Monsieur de la Jarry," said a servant, opening the door.

"A sporting companion?" said Lectoure.

"No," replied M. de Nozay; "he is a traveller."

"Ah! ah!" exclaimed Lectoure, with an accent which announced that the newly arrived personage was to be the subject of a new attack. He had hardly made the ejaculation, when the person announced entered the room, muffled up in a Polish dress, lined with fur.

"Ah! my dear La Jarry," cried Emanuel, advancing to meet him, and holding out his hand to him, "but how you are be-furred! Upon my honor, you look like the Czar Peter."

"It is," replied La Jarry, shivering, although the weather was by no means cold, "because, when one arrives from Naples—perrrrrou!"

"Ah! the gentleman has arrived from Naples," said Lectoure, joining in the conversation.

"Direct, sir."

"Did you ascend Vesuvius, sir?"

"No. I was satisfied with looking at it from my window. And then," continued the traveller, with a tone of contempt, most humiliating to the volcano, "Vesuvius is not the most curious thing that is to be seen at Naples. A mountain that smokes? my chimney does as much, when the wind is in the wrong quarter,—and besides Madame La Jarry was dreadfully alarmed at the idea of an eruption."

"But of course you visited the Grotto del Cane?" continued Lectoure.

"To what purpose?" rejoined La Jarry; "to see an animal that has vapors—give a pill to the first poodle that passes, and he will do as much. And then, Madame La Jarry has quite a passion for dogs, and it would have given her pain to witness so cruel an exhibition."

"I hope, however, that a man of science, like yourself," said Emanuel, bowing, "did not neglect the Solfatara."

"Who, I—I would not set my foot there. I can very easily imagine what three or four acres of sulphur looks like, the sole produce of which is a few millions of matches. Moreover, Madame La Jarry cannot support the odour of sulphur."

"What do you think of our new friend?" said Emanuel, leading Lectoure into the room in which the contract was to be signed.

"I know not whether it is because I saw the other first, but I decidedly prefer Nozay."

The door again opened, and the servant loudly announced, "Monsieur Paul."

"Eh!" exclaimed Emanuel, turning round.

"Who is this?" inquired Lectoure, listlessly, "another country neighbour?"

"No; this is quite another sort of person," replied Emanuel, with agitation. "How does this man dare to present himself here?"

"Ah! ah! a plebeian—eh? a common fellow, is he not? but rich, I suppose. No—a poet? musician? painter? well, I can assure you, Emanuel, that they are beginning to receive this sort of people—that accursed philosophy has confounded every thing. It cannot be helped, my dear fellow, we must courageously make up our minds to it—we have come to that. An artist sits down by a great noble, elbows him, touches the corner of his hat to him, remains seated when the other rises—they converse together on court matters—they jest, they joke, they squabble, it is bon ton though decidedly bad taste."

"You are mistaken, Lectoure," replied Emanuel; "he is neither poet, painter, or musician: he is a man to whom I must speak alone. Just lead off Nozay, while I do the same with La Jarry."

Upon this, the two young gentlemen took each of the country neighbours by the arm, and drew them away into another room, talking of shooting and travelling. The side door through which they went out, had scarcely closed upon them, when Paul appeared at the principal one. He went into the room he already knew, each corner of which concealed a door—the one led to a library, the other to the room in which he had been shut up on his first visit, awaiting the result of the conference between Marguerite and Emanuel, and then approaching the table, he remained there for a moment, looking attentively at the two doors, as though he had expected to see one of them opened. His hope was not fallacious. In a few moments, that of the library was opened, and he perceived a white form standing within it; he rushed towards it.

"Is it you, Marguerite?" said he.

"Yes," replied a trembling voice.

"Well?"

"I told him all?"

"And—"

"And in ten minutes the contract is to be signed."

"I suspected as much—he is a miserable wretch."

"What's to be done?" cried the young girl.

"Take courage, Marguerite."

"Courage—oh! it now fails me entirely."

"There is that which will restore it," said Paul, handing her a letter.

"What does this letter contain?"

"The name of the village in which you will find your son, and the name of the woman in whose house he has been concealed."

"My son! oh! you are my guardian angel," cried Marguerite, endeavoring to kiss the hand which held the paper to her.

"Silence! someone is coming—whatever may happen, you will find one at Achards."

Marguerite suddenly closed the door without replying to

him, for she had heard: the sound of her brother's footsteps. Paul turned round, and went to meet him, which he did, near the table.

"I expected you at another time, sir, and in less numerous company," said Emanuel, who was the first to speak.

"It appears to me that we are alone at this moment," said Paul, glancing around the room.

"Yes, but it is here that the contract is to be signed, and in an instant this room will be full."

"But many things may be said in an instant, count."

"You are right, sir, but you must meet a man who does not require more than an instant to comprehend them."

"I am listening," said Paul.

"You spoke to me of letters," rejoined Emanuel, drawing nearer to him, and lowering his voice.

"It is true," said Paul, with the same calmness.

"You fixed a price upon those letters?"

"That is also true."

"Well, then! if you are a man of honor, for that price, for the sum enclosed in this pocket-book, you ought now to be prepared to give them up."

"Yes, sir, yes," replied Paul, "the case stood thus, as long as I believed your sister, forgetful of the vows she had made, the fault she had committed, and even the child to which she had given birth, was seconding your ambition by her perjury. Then, I thought it would be a sufficiently bitter fate for the poor child to enter upon life without a name and without a family, not to allow him to enter it without a fortune also, and I then demanded of you, it is true, that sum in exchange for the letters in my possession. But now the state of things is altered, sir. I saw your sister throw herself upon her knees before you, I heard her entreat you not to force her into this infamous marriage, and neither prayers, nor tears, nor supplications could make any impression on your heart. It is now for me, for me who hold your honor, and the honor of your family within my hands, it is for me to save the mother from despair, as I would have saved the child from penury and misery. Those letters, sir, shall be delivered to you, when you shall, upon this table, instead of signing the marriage contract of your sister with the Baron de Lectoure, sign that of Mademoiselle Marguerite d'Auray with Anatole de Lusignan."

"Never, sir, never!"

"You shall not have them, excepting on that condition, count."

"Oh! I shall, perhaps, find some mode of compiling you to return them."

"I know not any," coldly replied Paul.

"Will you, sir, deliver those letters to me!"

"Count," replied Paul, with an expression of countenance, which, under the circumstances, was perfectly inexplicable to Emanuel, "count, listen to me?"

"Will you return me those letters, sir?"

"Count—"

"Yes, or no!"

"No!" said Paul, calmly.

"Well then, sir, you wear a sword, as I do; we are both gentlemen, or rather I would believe you to be such; let us leave the house together, and one of us shall return alone, and he, being unfettered and powerful from the death of the other, shall then do as he best pleases."

"I regret I cannot accept the offer, count."

"How? you wear that uniform, that cross upon your breast, by your side that sword, and you refuse a duel."

"Yes, Emanuel, I do refuse it, because I cannot raise my sword against you, count—believe me, I entreat you."

"You cannot fight with me!"

"I cannot, upon my honor."

"You cannot fight with me, you say?"

"At this moment a person who had entered the room without being perceived, burst into a loud laugh, close behind the two young men. Paul and Emanuel turned hastily round. Lectoure was standing close to them.

"But," said Paul, pointing to Lectoure, "I can fight with him, for he is a miserable and infamous wretch."

A burning blush passed over Lectoure's features, like the reflection of a flame. He made a step towards Paul, and then stopped.

"It is well, sir," said he; "send your second to Emanuel and they can arrange this matter."

"You will understand that between us the affair is merely deferred," said Emanuel, to Paul.

"Silence!" replied Paul, "they are announcing your mother."

"Yes, silence, and to-morrow we meet again. Lectoure," added Emanuel, "let us go to receive my mother."

Paul looked silently at the young men as they retired, and then he entered the small room in which he had before been concealed.

CHAPTER XIII.—THE CONTRACT.

Listen to me and heed me!
If this contract
Thou holdst me to, abide thou the result!
Answer to heaven for what I suffer! act!
Prepare thyself for such calamity
To fall on me, and those whose evil
Have linked them with me, as no past mishap,
However rare and marvellously Sad,
Can parallel.

Knowles—The Hunchback.

At the moment that Paul went into the study, the marchioness appeared at the door of the drawing-room, followed by the notary, and the several persons who had been invited to be present at the signing of the contract. Notwithstanding the nature of the meeting, the marchioness had not considered it proper to lay aside, even for one evening, her mourning garments, and dressed in complete black, as she had been always during twenty years, she came into the room a few moments before the marquis. None of the persons present, not even his son, had seen the marquis for many years. Such attention was in those days paid to ancient forms, that the marchioness would not allow the marriage contract of her daughter to be signed, without the head of the family, although deprived of reason, being present; at the ceremony. However little accustomed Lectoure was to feel intimidated, the marchioness produced upon him the effect which she did on every one that approached her, and on seeing her enter the room with so grave and dignified an aspect, he bowed to her with a feeling of profound respect.

"I am grateful to you, gentlemen," said the marchioness, bowing to the persons who accompanied her, "for the honor you have been pleased to confer upon me, by being present at the betrothal of Mademoiselle Marguerite d'Auray, with the Baron de Lectoure. I, in consequence, was desirous that the marquis, although suffering from illness, should also be present at this meeting, to thank you at least by his presence, if he cannot do so verbally. You are all aware of his unfortunate malady, and you will, therefore, not be astonished, should some disjointed words—"

"Yes, madam," said Lectoure, interrupting her, "we know the misfortune which has befallen him, and we admire the devoted wife, who for twenty years has borne half the weight of this sad visitation."

"You see, madam," said Emanuel, addressing in his turn, and kissing the hand of his mother, "all the world bows down in admiration of your conjugal piety."

"Where is Marguerite?" murmured the marchioness, in a hair whisper.

"She was here not a moment ago," said Emanuel. "Let her know that we are all assembled," rejoined the marchioness, in the same tone.

A servant then announced "the Marquis d'Auray." All present drew to one side, so as to leave free passage from the door, and all eyes were directed to the spot at which this new personage was to appear. It was not long before their curiosity was satisfied; the marquis came in almost immediately, supported by two servants.

He was an old man, whose countenance, notwithstanding that the traces of suffering had deeply furrowed it, still retained that noble and dignified appearance which had rendered him one of the most distinguished men of the court of Louis XV. His large, hollow, and feverish eyes, glanced around the assembly with a strange expression of astonishment. He was dressed in his costume of Steward of the Household, wore the order of the Holy Ghost suspended from his neck, and that of St. Louis, at his button hole. He advanced slowly, and without uttering a word. The two servants led him forward amid the most profound silence, to an arm-chair, in which he seated himself, and the servants left the room. The marchioness then placed herself at his right hand. The notary opened the portfolio, drew from it the marriage contract and read it aloud. The marquis and the marchioness made over the sum of five hundred thousand francs to Lectoure, and gave a like sum to Marguerite, as her dowry.

During the whole of the time occupied by the reading of the contract, the marchioness, notwithstanding her great self command, had betrayed some symptoms of uneasiness. But just at the moment when the notary had placed the contract open on the table, Emanuel returned and approached his mother.

"And Marguerite?" said the marchioness.

"She will be here instantly."

"Madam," murmured Marguerite, half opening the door, and clasping her hands.

The marchioness pretended not to hear her, and pointed with her finger at the pen.

"Baron, it is you who are first to sign."

Lectoure immediately approached the table and signed the contract.

"Madam!" cried Marguerite, in a tone of supplication, and advancing one step toward her mother.

"Pass the pen to your betrothed, Baron," said the marchioness.

The Baron walked round the table, and drew near to Marguerite.

"Madam!" again cried the latter, with an accent so melancholy, that it struck to the heart of every person present, and even the marquis himself raised his head.

"Sign!" said the marchioness, pointing to the marriage contract.

"Oh! my father! my father!" exclaimed Marguerite throwing herself at the feet of the marquis.

"What does this mean?" said the marchioness, leaning upon the arm of the marquis' chair, and bending over him, "are you mad, mademoiselle?"

"My father! oh! my father!" again cried Marguerite, throwing her arms around him, "my father, have pity, save your daughter!"

"Marguerite!" murmured the marchioness, in a

threatening accent.

"Madam!" replied Marguerite, "I cannot address myself to you—permit me, then, to implore my father's pity; unless," she added, pointing to the notary with a firm and determined gesture, "you would prefer my invoking the protection of the law."

"Come, come," said the marchioness, rising, and in a tone of bitter irony, "this is a family scene, and which, although highly interesting to near relations, must be sufficiently tedious to strangers. Gentlemen, you will find refreshments in the adjoining rooms. My son, conduct these gentlemen, and do the honors. Baron, I must beg your pardon for a short time." Emanuel and Lectoure bowed in silence and withdrew, followed by all the company. The marchioness remained motionless until the last of them had withdrawn, and then she closed all the doors leading into the room, when, returning to the marquis, whom Marguerite still held clasped in her arms.

"And now," said she, "that there is no one present excepting those who have the right to lay their commands upon you, sign that paper, mademoiselle, or leave the room."

"For pity's sake, madam, for pity's sake, do not compel me to commit so infamous an act!"

"Have you not heard me?" said the marchioness, giving to her voice an imperative tone, which she thought impossible to be resisted, "or must I repeat my words? 'Sign, or leave the room.'"

"Oh! my father!" cried Marguerite, "mercy! mercy! No,

it shall not be said, that after having been banished from my father's presence for ten years, I was torn from his arms the first time I again beheld him—and that, before he had recognized me, before he has embraced me. Oh! father! father!—it is I, it is your daughter!"

"What is that voice that is imploring me?" murmured the marquis. "Who is this child who calls me father?"

"That voice," said the marchioness, seizing the arm of her daughter, "is a voice that is raised against the rights of nature. That child is a rebellious daughter."

"My father!" cried Marguerite imploringly, "look at me. Oh! my father, save me I defend me! I am Marguerite."

"Marguerite? Marguerite?" stammered the marquis, "I had formerly a child of that name."

"It is I! it is I!" rejoined Marguerite: "I am your child—I am your daughter."

"There are no children but those who obey. Obey! and you will then have the right to call yourself our daughter," rejoined the marchioness.

"To you, my father, yes,—to you I am ready to obey. But you do not command this sacrifice! you do not wish that I should be unhappy—unhappy even to despair—unhappy even to death."

"Come! come!" said the marquis holding her in his turn, and pressing her to his heart. "Oh! this is a delicious and unknown feeling to me. And now—wait! wait!" He pressed his hand to his forehead. "It seems to me that I recollect."

"Sir!" cried the marchioness, "tell her that she ought to

obey; that the malediction of God awaits rebellious children. Tell her that, rather than to encourage her in her impiety!"

The marquis slowly raised his head, and fixed his piercing eyes upon his wife, and then slowly pronounced the following words: "Take care! madam, take care. Have I not told you that I begin to remember!" and then again bending down his head to that of Marguerite, so that his grey hairs mingled with the dark tresses, of his daughter—"Speak—speak!" said he, "what is it that disturbs you, my child—tell me all."

"Oh! I am most unhappy!"

"Everybody, then, is unhappy here," exclaimed the marquis, "whether their hair be grey or black—an old man or a child.. Oh! and I also—I am unhappy—be assured.

"Sir, go up stairs into your room again: you must," said the marchioness.

"Yes, that I may again be face to face with you; shut up like a prisoner! That may be very well, when I am mad."

"Yes, yes, my father, you are right. My mother has devoted herself to you long enough; it is now time that your daughter should perform that duty. Take me with you, father. I will not leave you day or night. You will only have to make a sign, to utter a word, and I will serve you on my knees."

"Oh! you would not have the strength to do it."

"Yes, yes, my father, I will—as truly as I am your daughter."

The marchioness wrung her hands with impatience.

"If you are my daughter, how is it that I have not seen you for ten years?"

"Because I was told that you would not see me, my father;

160

because they told me that you did not love me."

"You were told that I would not see you—not see that angel face!" said he, taking her head between his hands, and looking at her with intense auction; "they told you that—they told you that a poor condemned soul did not wish for heaven! Who was it, then, that told you a father would not see his child? Who has dared to say, child, your father loves you not?"

"I!——" said the marchioness, again endeavoring to take Marguerite from her father's arms.

"You!" exclaimed the marquis, interrupting her: "it was you? To you then, has been confided the fatal mission of deceiving me in all my affections. All my griefs, then, must find their source in you? You wish, then, now to break the father's heart, as twenty years ago, you did that of the husband."

"You are delirious, sir," said the marchioness, loosing the arm of her daughter; and going to the right of the marquis, she whispered—"be silent!"

"No, madam, no, I am not now delirious," replied the marquis, "No! no! Say rather, say that,—and it will be the truth,—say that I am now between an angel who would recall me to reason, and a demon who wishes me again to become insane. No! No! I am not mad. Do you wish that I should prove it to you?" He rose, supporting himself on the arms of his chair. "Must I speak to you of letters, of adultery, of a duel?"

"I say," said the marchioness, grasping his arm, "I tell

you that you are more forsaken by heaven than ever, when you utter such things, without reflecting as to whose ears are listening. Cast down your eyes, sir—look who is standing yonder, and then dare assert that you are not mad!"

"You are right;" said the marquis, falling back in his chair. "Your mother is right," continued he, addressing Marguerite—"I am mad, and you must not believe what I say, but what she says. Your mother is devotedness, virtue itself, and therefore, she has not sleepless nights, nor remorse, nor madness. What does your mother wish?"

"My misery, father; my everlasting misery."

"And how can I prevent this misery?" said the unhappy old man, with a most heart-rending anguish; "how can I, a poor, insane old man, prevent it? who thinks he always sees the blood issuing from a wound—who thinks he constantly hears a voice proceeding from a tomb!"

"Oh you can do all; say but one word and I am saved! They wish me to marry—"

The marquis listlessly reclined his head on the back of his chair.

"Listen to me! they wish to marry me to a man whom I do not love—do you understand me?—to a wretch!—and you have been brought here—placed in that arm-chair, before the table—you, you my father! to sign this infamous contract—this contract which I now hand to you."

"Without consulting me," said the marquis, taking the contract; "without asking me whether I will, or I will not! Do they believe me dead? And if they think me dead, do they fear me less than they would a spectre? This marriage would cause your misery, you say?"

"My eternal misery!" exclaimed Marguerite. "The marriage, then, shall not take place."

"I have pledged your word and mine," said the marchioness, and with the more energy, that she felt her influence over her husband about to escape her.

"This marriage, I tell you, shall not take place!" replied the marquis, in a tone louder than that of his wife. "It is too dreadful a thing," continued he, in a gloomy sepulchral tone, "to be permitted. A marriage in which a wife loves not her husband—why, it causes madness! As to myself, the marchioness has always loved me, and loved me faithfully— that which drove me mad—oh! that was a different matter."

A flash of diabolical joy shot from the eyes of the marchioness, for she at once saw from the violence of the expressions used by her husband, and the terror depicted on his features, that his insanity was about to return.

"This contract," said the marquis, and he raised it in his hands as if about to tear it.

The marchioness eagerly caught his hand. Marguerite appeared to be hanging by a thread between heaven and hell.

"That which drives me mad!" reiterated the marquis, "is a tomb which widely opens, a spectre that issues from the earth, it is a phantom that speaks to me, and says—"

"Your life is in my hands!" murmured the marchioness in his ear, repeating the last words of the dying Morlaix: "I could take it."

"Do you hear that?" cried the marquis, rising, and as if about to rush from the room.

"My father! oh! my father! recall your senses; there is no tomb, there is no spectre, there is no phantom; those words were uttered by the marchioness."

"But I wish you to live," continued the latter, concluding the sentence she had begun, "to forgive me as I forgive you."

"Pardon, Morlaix, pardon!" cried the marquis, falling back in his arm-chair, his hair standing on end with terror, and the perspiration streaming from his forehead.

"Oh! father! father!"

"You see that your father is altogether deranged," said the marchioness, triumphantly; "say no more to him."

"Oh!" cried Marguerite, "God will, I trust perform a miracle! My love, my caresses, my tears, will restore him to reason."

"Make the attempt," replied the marchioness, coldly, abandoning to her care the marquis, who was powerless, speechless, and almost without consciousness.

"Oh! my poor father!" exclaimed Marguerite, in a tone of agony.

The marquis remained perfectly impassible.

"Sir!" said the marchioness, in an imperative manner.

"Eh! eh!" cried the marquis, shuddering.

"Save me! oh! save me, father!" cried Marguerite, wringing her hands, and throwing herself back in despair.

"Take this pen and sign," said the marchioness, "you must—it is my will."

"Now, I am lost indeed!" cried Marguerite, overwhelmed with terror, and feeling that she had no longer strength to continue the struggle.

But at the moment that the marquis, overpowered, had written the first letters of his name; when the marchioness was congratulating herself on the victory she had obtained, and Marguerite was about to leave the room in despair, an unexpected incident suddenly changed the scene. The door of the study opened, and Paul, who had been anxiously watching, though invisibly, the whole of this terrible conflict, issued from it.

"Madam," said he, "one word before this contract is signed!"

"Who is it calls me!" said the marchioness, endeavoring to distinguish in the distance that separated them, the person who had thus spoken, and who stood in a dark corner of the room.

"I know that voice!" exclaimed the marquis, shuddering, as if seared by a red-hot iron.

Paul advanced three paces, and the light from the lustre hanging in the centre of the room fell full upon him.

"Is it a spectre?" cried the marchioness, in her turn, struck with the resemblance of the youth who stood before her to her former lover.

"I know that face!" cried the marquis, believing that he saw the man whom he had killed.

"My God! my God! protect me," stammered Marguerite, raising her eyes and hands to heaven.

"Morlaix! Morlaix!" said the marquis, rising and advancing toward Paul, "Morlaix!—pardon! mercy!" and he fell at full length upon the floor.

"My father!" cried Marguerite, rushing to his assistance.

At that moment a servant entered the room, with terror in his looks, and addressing the marchioness said—

"Madam, Achard has sent to request that the priest and the doctor of the castle, may instantly be ordered to attend him—he is dying."

"Tell him," replied the marchioness, pointing to her husband, whom Marguerite was vainly endeavoring to restore to consciousness, "that they are both obliged to remain here to attend upon the marquis."

CHAPTER XIV.—RELIGIOUS CONVICTION.

And this our life, exempt from public haunt,
Finds tongues in trees, books in the running brooks,
Sermons in stones, and good in every thing.

Shakespeare.

As has been seen by the end of the preceding chapter, God, by one of those extraordinary combinations, which short-sighted man almost always attributes to chance, had summoned to his presence, and almost at the same moment, the souls of the noble Marquis d'Auray, and the poor low-born Achard. We have seen that the former, struck by the sight of Paul, the living portrait of his father, as if by a thunderbolt, fell at the feet of the young man, who was himself terrified at the effect his appearance had produced.

As to Achard, the circumstances which had hastened his death, although differing in their nature, and from very opposite feelings, had arisen from the same fatal causes, and had been brought about by the same individual. The sight of Paul had created direful emotions in the breasts both of the marquis and Achard. On the former from excess of terror, on the latter from excess of joy.

During the day which had preceded the intended signing of the contract, Achard had felt himself more feeble than usual. Notwithstanding this, he had not neglected in the evening to crawl to his master's grave, there to put up his accustomed prayer. Thence he had observed with a devotion more profound than ever, that ever new and splendid spectacle, the sun sinking into the ocean. He had followed the decline of its enpurpled light, and as though the vast torch of the world had drawn his soul toward it, he had felt his strength extinguished with its last rays; so that when the servant from the castle came in the evening at the accustomed hour to receive his orders, not finding him in his house, had sought for him without the park, and as it was well known that he generally walked in that direction, found him lying extended at the foot of the great oak tree, upon the grave of his master, and deprived of consciousness. Thus did he remain constant to the last in that religious devotedness he had vowed to his master's tomb, and which had been the exclusive feeling of the last years of his life.

The servant took him in his arms, and carried him into his house; and then, terrified at the unexpected accident, had hastened to the marchioness to inform her that Achard required the attendance of a physician and a priest, which message was delivered to her by the servant then in waiting, to which the marchioness refused to accede, under the pretext that they were required as urgently by the marquis as the old servant, and that superiority of rank, powerful, even when at the point of death, gave her husband the right of first employing.

But the intelligence which had been announced to the marchioness at the moment of that dreadful agony, into which their varying interests and varying passions had thrown the actors in this family drama, of which we have become the historian, this intelligence, we say, was heard by Paul. Conceiving that the signature of the contract had now become impossible from the state of the marquis, he had only allowed himself time to whisper to Marguerite, that should she need his assistance, she would find him at Achard's cottage, and then he rushed into the park, and winding his way amid its serpentine walks and thickets, with the skill of a sear man, who reads his path in the starry firmament, he soon reached the house, entered it panting from his rapid course, and found Achard just as he was recovering from his fainting fit, and clasped him in his arms. The delight of again seeing him renewed the strength of the old man, who now felt certain of having a friendly hand to close his eyes.

"Oh! it is you—it is you!" exclaimed the old man.

"I did not hope to see you again."

"And could you possibly believe that I should have been apprized of the state in which you were, and that I would not instantly fly to your assistance?"

"But I knew not where to find you—where I could send to tell you that I wished once more to see you before I died."

"I was at the castle, father, where I learned that you were dangerously ill, and I hastened hither."

"And how was it that you were at the castle?" said the old man, with amazement.

Paul related to him all that had occurred.

"Eternal Providence!" cried the old man, when Paul had concluded his recital, "how hidden and inevitable are thy decrees. Thou, who, after twenty years, hast conducted this youth to the cradle of his infancy, and hast killed the assassin of the father, by the mere aspect of the son!"

"Yes, yes, thus it happens," replied Paul, "and it is Providence, also, who conducts me to you, that I might save you. For I heard them refuse to send you the physician and the priest."

"According to common justice," rejoined Achard, "they might have made a fair division. The marquis, who fears death, might have retained the physician, while to me who am tired of life, they might have sent the priest."

"I can go on horseback," said Paul, "and in less than an hour—"

"In an hour it would be too late," said the dying man, in an enfeebled voice, "a priest! a priest only—I ask but for a priest."

"Father," replied Paul, "in his sacred functions, I know I cannot supply his place; but we can speak of God, of his greatness and his goodness."

"Yes, but let us first finish with the things of this earth, that we may then be able to turn our thoughts wholly to those of heaven. You say that, like myself, the marquis is dying."

"I left him at the last agony."

"You know, that immediately after his death, the papers which are deposited in that closet, and which prove your birth, are yours by right."

"I know it."

"If I die before the marquis, to whom can I confide them?" The old man sat up and pointed to a key hanging at the head of his bed. "You will take that key, you will open the closet—in it you will find a casket. You are a man of honor. Swear to me that you will not open that casket until the marquis shall be dead."

"I swear it," said Paul solemnly, and extending his hand towards the crucifix hanging at the head of the bed.

"'Tis well," replied Achard; "now I shall die in peace."

"You may do so, for the son holds your hand in this world, and the father stretches out his towards you from heaven!"

"Do you believe, my child, that he will be satisfied with my fidelity?"

"No king was ever so faithfully obeyed during life, as he has been since his death."

"Yes," murmured the old man, in a gloomy tone, "I was but too exact in following his orders. I ought not to have suffered the duel to have taken place; I ought to have refused attending it as a witness. Hear me, Paul; it is this that I wished to have said to a priest, for it is the only thing that weighs upon my conscience: listen: there have been moments of doubt, during which, I have regarded this solitary duel as an assassination. In that case, Paul, oh! in that case, I have not only been a witness, but an accomplice!"

"Oh! my second father," replied Paul, "I know not whether the laws of earth are always in accordance with the laws of heaven, and whether honor as it is considered by man, would be a virtue in the eyes of the Lord; I know not whether our holy church, an enemy to bloodshed, permits that the injured should attempt with his own hands, to avenge the wrongs inflicted upon him by attacking his injurer, and if in that case, the judgment of heaven directs the pistol ball or the sword's point. These are questions not to be decided by reasoning, but by conscience. Well, then, my conscience tells me, that situated as you were, I should have done precisely as you did. Should conscience in this case mislead me, it also misled you, and in this view of the matter, I have a greater right than a priest, to absolve you; and in my name, and in that of my father, I pardon you."

"Thanks! thanks!" cried the old man, pressing the hands of Paul; "thanks, for these words, pour consolation into the soul of a dying man. Remorse is a dreadful thing! remorse would lead one to believe that there exists no God. For without a judge there can be no judgment."

"Listen to me," said Paul, in that poetic and solemn accent, which was peculiar to him: "I also have often doubted in the existence of a God: isolated and lost in the wide world, without family, and without a single friend, I sought for support in the Lord, and I asked of every thing that encircled me, some proof of his existence. Often have I arrested my steps at the foot of one of these crosses, erected by the road side, and with my eyes fixed upon the Saviour, I demanded, and with tears, to be assured of his existence, and divine mission; I prayed that his eyes would deign to look upon me: that one drop of blood might fall from his wound, or that a sigh might issue from his lips. The crucifix remained motionless, and I arose, my heart being overcome with despair, saying—'did I but know where I could find my father's tomb, I would question him as Hamlet did the ghost, and he would perhaps answer me!'"

"Poor child!"

"Then would I enter a church," continued Paul, "one of those churches of the north, gloomy, religious, Christian! And I would feel myself borne down with sorrow; but sorrow is not faith! I approached the altar; I threw myself upon my knees before the tabernacle, in which God dwells; I bowed my head till it touched the marble of the steps; and when I had thus remained prostrated for hours and lost in doubt, I raised my head, hoping that the God I was seeking would at length manifest his presence to me by a ray of his glory, or by some dazzling proof of his power. But the church remained gloomy, as the cross had remained motionless. And I would then rush from its porches with insensate haste, crying, 'Lord! Lord! didst thou exist, thou would reveal thyself to man. It is thy will, then, that men should doubt, since thou canst reveal thyself to them, but dost not.'"

"Beware of what you are saying, Paul," cried the old man: "beware that the doubt thy heart contains do not attaint mine! Thou hast time left to thee to believe, whereas, I—I am about to die."

"Wait, father, wait!" continued Paul, with softened voice, and placid features. "I have not told you all. It was then, that I said to myself, 'the crucifix by the road side, the churches of the cities are but the work of man. Let us seek God, in God's own works.' From that moment, my father, began that wandering life, which will remain an eternal mystery, known only to the heavens, the ocean, and myself—it led me into the solitary wilds of America, for I thought the newer a world was, the more freshly would it retain the impress of God's hand. I did not deceive myself. There, often in those virgin forests, into which I was perhaps the first who had ever penetrated; with no shelter, but the heavens, no couch, but the earth, absorbed by one sole thought, I have listened to the thousand noises of a world about to sleep, and nature when awakening. For a long time, did I still remain without comprehending that unknown tongue, formed by the mingling of the murmur of rivers, the vapor of the lakes, the rustling of the forest, and the perfume of flowers. Finally, the veil which had obscured my eyes, and the weight which had oppressed my heart, was little by little removed; and from that time, I began to believe that these noises of evening, and of approaching day, were but one universal hymn, by which created things expressed their gratitude to the Creator."

"Almighty God!" cried the dying man, clasping his hands, and raising his eyes to heaven, with an expression of holy faith, "I cried to you from the bottomless pit, and you heard me in my distress; oh! my God I I thank thee."

"Then," continued Paul, with still increasing enthusiasm, "then, I sought upon the ocean, that full conviction which earth had refused to me. The earth is but a span—the ocean is immensity! The ocean is, after God himself, the grandest, the most powerful object in the universe. I have heard the ocean roar like a chafed lion, and then at the voice of its master, become tranquil as a submissive dog; I have seen it rise like a Titan, to scale the heavens; and then beneath the whip of the tempest, moan like a weeping infant. I have seen it dashing its waves to meet the lightning, and endeavoring to quench the thunder with its foam; and then become smooth as a mirror, and reflect even the smallest star in the heavens. Upon the land, I had become convinced of God's existence, upon the ocean, I recognised his power. In the solitary wilds, as Moses, I had heard the voice of the Lord, but during the tempest, I saw him, as did Ezekiel, riding upon the wings of the storm. Thenceforward, my father, thenceforward, all doubt was driven from my mind, and from the evening on which I witnessed the first hurricane, I believed, and prayed."

"I believe in God, the Father Almighty, maker of Heaven and Earth," said the dying man, with ardent faith; and he continued thus the symbol of the apostles to the last word.

Paul listened to him in silence, with his eyes raised to heaven, and when he had concluded, said—

"It is not thus, that a priest would have spoken to you, my father, for I have spoken to you as a seaman, and with a voice more accustomed to pronounce words of death than consolation. Forgive me, father, forgive me for it."

"You have made me pray, and believe as you do," said the old man; "tell me, then, what more could a priest have done? What you have said is plain and grand—let me reflect on what you have said."

"Listen!" said Paul, shuddering, "What is it?"

"Did you not hear?"

"No."

175

"I thought that a voice of some one in distress called to me—there again—do you not hear it?—now, again!—It is the voice of Marguerite."

"Go to her instantly," replied the old man; "I need to be alone."

Paul rushed into the adjoining room, and as he entered it he heard his name again repeated, and close to the door of the cottage. Then, running to the door he anxiously opened it, and found Marguerite upon the threshold, her strength having failed her, and she had fallen upon her knees.

"Save me! save me!" she cried, with an expression of profound terror, on perceiving Paul, and clasped his knees.

CHAPTER XV.—THE PAPERS.

Mercy from him!
And how can I expect it?
By what right
Can I demand he should withhold his claim,
The proofs once in his power?

—*Anonymous.*

Paul ran to Marguerite, and caught her in his arms; she was pale and icy cold. He carried her into the first room, placed her in an arm chair, returned to the door which had remained open, and closed it, and then hastened back.

"What is it that so terrifies you? who is pursuing you? and how does it happen that you come here at this unusual hour?"

"Oh!" exclaimed Marguerite, "at any hour, whether by day or night, I should have flown as long as the earth would have borne me! I should have flown till I had found some heart in which I could have poured forth my sorrows, an arm capable of defending me. Paul! Paul! my father is dead?"

"Poor child!" said Paul, pressing Marguerite to his heart, "who flies from one house of death to fall into another; who leaves death in the castle, to find it in the cottage."

"Yes, yes!" cried Marguerite rising, still trembling with terror, and convulsively pressing Paul's arm. "Death is yonder, and I find death here! but yonder it is attended with despair and fear, while here it is met with tranquillity and hope. Oh!

177

Paul! Paul! had you but seen that which I have seen!"

"Tell me all that happened."

"You saw the terrible effect produced by your appearance, and the mere sound of your voice?"

"Yes, I saw that."

"They carried him still fainting and speechless into his own room."

"It was to your mother that I spoke," said Paul, "and he heard me; I could not foresee it would so much have terrified him."

"You full well know all that had passed, for you must have heard from the room in which you were concealed, every word we uttered. My father, my poor father, had recognized me, and I, seeing him thus, could, not repress my uneasiness: notwithstanding the risk I ran of irritating my mother, I went up to his room—the door was locked; I knocked softly at it. He had recovered his senses, for I heard a faint voice asking 'who was there?'"

"And your mother?" said Paul eagerly.

"My mother," replied Marguerite, "was no longer there, and she had locked him in as she would have done to a child; but when he had recognized my voice, when I had told him that it was his daughter Marguerite who wished to see him, he told me that I could get into the room by going down stairs again, and that in the study I should find a private staircase which led to it. A minute afterwards, I was kneeling by his bedside, and he gave me his blessing. Yes, Paul, I received his blessing before he died, his paternal benediction, which

I trust will bring down the blessing of God upon my head."

"Yes," said Paul, "God will pardon you; you may now feel tranquil. Weep for your father, Marguerite, but weep no longer for yourself, for you are saved."

"You have heard nothing yet, Paul!" exclaimed Marguerite. "Hear me still."

"Proceed!"

"At the very moment when I was kneeling, kissing the hand of my father, and thanking him for the relief he had afforded my afflicted mind, I heard my mothers footstep on the staircase. I recognized her voice, and my father also recognized it, for he again embraced me, and made a sign to me to leave him. I obeyed him, but such was my terror and confusion, that I mistook the door, and instead of the staircase by which I had ascended, I found myself in a small cabinet which had no issue. I felt all around its walls, but could find no door. I was compelled to remain there. I then heard my mother, accompanied by the priest, entering my father's room—I restrained my breathing, fearing that she should hear me. I saw then through the glass window of the door, and I assure you, Paul, that she was paler than my father who was about to die."

"Gracious heaven!" murmured Paul.

"The priest seated himself by the bed-side," continued Marguerite, so terrified that she pressed still closer against Paul; "my mother remained standing at the foot of the bed—I was there, just opposite to them, compelled to remain a witness of that mournful spectacle, without the means of retreat!—a daughter, obliged to hear the dying confession of her father!—was it not horrible? I fell upon my knees, closing my eyes that I might not see—praying that I might not hear—and yet in spite of myself—and this I swear to you, Paul—I saw and I heard—Oh! what I then heard, can never be obliterated from my memory—I saw my father, whose recollections seemed to inspire him with a feverish strength, sit up in his bed, the paleness of death imprinted on his face. I heard him—I heard him pronounce the words, a duel—adultery—assassination!—and at each word he uttered, I saw my mother turn pale—and paler even than before—and I heard her raise her voice so that it might drown the voice of the dying man, saying to the priest: 'believe him not—believe him not, reverend father; what he says is false—or rather, he is mad, he knows not what he says—believe him not!' Oh! Paul, it was a dreadful spectacle, an impious sacrilege; a cold perspiration stood upon my forehead, and I fainted."

"Justice of Heaven!" cried Paul. "I know not how long I remained without consciousness. When I recovered my senses, the room was as silent as the tomb. My mother and the priest had disappeared, and two wax lights were burning near my father. I opened the door of the cabinet, and cast my eyes on the bed; it appeared to me that I could distinguish beneath the sheet which completely covered it, the stiffened form of a corpse. I divined that all was over! I remained motionless, divided between the funereal awe which such a sight inspired, and the pious desire of raising the covering to kiss once more before he should be inclosed in his coffin, the venerable forehead of my dear father. Fear, however, overcame every other feeling—an ice-like mortal, and invincible terror drove me from the room. I flew down the staircase, I know not how, but I believe without touching a single step,—I fled across the rooms and through the corridors, till the freshness of the air convinced me that I had left the castle. I fled, completely unconscious of whither my steps were leading me, until I remembered you had told me I should find you here. A secret instinct—tell me what it was—for I cannot myself comprehend it, had led me in this direction. It appeared to me that I was pursued by shadows, horrid phantoms. At the corner of one of the avenues I thought— (had I then lost my senses?)—I thought I saw my mother, dressed all in black, and walking as noiselessly as a sceptre. Oh! then, then! terror lent me wings—I at first fled without knowing whither; after this my strength failed me, and it was then you heard my cries. I dragged myself along a few more paces, and fell motionless at this door; had you not opened it, I should have expired upon the spot, for I was so much terrified, that it appeared to me,"—then suddenly pausing, Marguerite trembled, and whispered to Paul, "Silence! do you not hear?"

"Yes," replied Paul, instantly extinguishing the lamp, "yes, yes—footsteps—I hear them also."

"Look! look!" cried Marguerite, concealing herself behind the curtain of the window, and throwing them around Paul at the same moment—"look! I was not mistaken—it was my mother."

The door had been opened, and the marchioness, pale as a spectre, entered the room slowly, closed the door after her, and locked it, and then without observing Paul and Marguerite, went into the second room where Achard was lying. She then walked up to his bed, as she had only a short time before to that of the marquis, only that she was not now accompanied by a priest.

"Who is there?" said Achard, drawing back one of the curtains of his bed.

"It is I," replied the marchioness, drawing back the other curtain.

"You, madam," cried the old man with terror; "for what purpose have you come to the bedside of a dying man?"

"I have come to make a proposal to him."

"One that will lose his soul! is it not?"

"To save it, on the contrary. There is only one thing in this world, Achard, of which you stand in need," rejoined the marchioness, bending down over the bed of the dying man, "and that is a priest."

"You refused to allow the one who is attached to the castle to attend me."

"In five minutes, if you wish it, he shall be here."

"Let him be sent then," said the old man, "and believe me there is not a moment to be lost. He must come quickly."

"But if I give you the peace of heaven, you will give me in exchange peace on earth."

"What can I do for you?" murmured the dying man, closing his eyes, that he might not see a woman whose looks chilled him.

"You stand in need of a priest, that you may die in peace," said the marchioness, "you know the gift I require, in order to exist in tranquillity."

"You would close heaven to me by a perjury."

"I would open it to you by a pardon."

"That pardon I have already received."

"And from whom?—"

"From him who, perhaps, had alone the right to grant it to me."

"Has Morlaix then descended from heaven?" asked the marchioness, in a tone in which there was almost as much terror as irony.

"No, madam," replied he, "but have you forgotten that he left a son upon this earth?"

"Then you have also seen him," exclaimed the marchioness.

"Yes," replied Achard.

"And you have told him all——"

"All!"

"And the papers which prove his birth?" asked the marchioness, with trembling anxiety.

"The marquis was not dead—the papers are still there."

"Achard!" cried the marchioness, falling upon her knees, by the bedside. "Achard! you will take pity on me?"

"You, on your knees, before me, madam?"

"Yes, old man," replied the marchioness, in a supplicating tone, "yes, I am on my knees before you—and I beg, I implore you, for you hold in your hands the honor of one of the most ancient families in France—my past, my future life! Those papers are my heart, my soul—they are more than this—they are my name—the name of my forefathers—of my children—and you well know all that I have suffered to preserve that name unsullied. Do you believe that I had not a heart as other women have? the feelings of a lover, of a wife, and of a mother? Well! I have overcome them all, one by one, and the struggle has been long. I am twenty years younger than you are, old man, I am still in the prime of life, and you are on the verge of the grave. Look, then, upon these hairs; they are even whiter than your own."

"What says she?" whispered Marguerite, who had softly crept to the door, and could see all that was passing in the inner room. "Gracious heaven!"

"Listen, listen, dear child," said Paul, "it is the Lord who permits that all shall be thus revealed."

"Yes, yes," murmured Achard, who was becoming weaker every moment. "Yes, you doubted the goodness of the Lord, you had forgotten that he had forgiven the adulterous woman—"

"Yes, but when she met with Christ, men were about to cast stones at her—men, who for twenty generations have been accustomed to revere our name, to honor our family— did they but learn, that which, thank heaven! has heretofore been hidden from them—would hear it uttered with shame and with contempt. I have so much suffered, that God will pardon me—but man! men are so implacable, that they will not pardon—moreover, am I alone exposed to their insults—

on either side, the cross I bear, have I not a child?—and is not the other that we speak of, the first-born? In the eyes of the law, is he not the son of the Marquis d'Auray? do you forget that he is the first-born, the head of the family? Do you not know, that in order to possess himself of the title, the estates, the fortune of the family of Auray, he has only to invoke the law? and then what would remain to Emanuel? The cross of the order of Malta—and to Marguerite?—a convent."

"Oh! yes, yes," whispered Marguerite, and stretching out her arms, toward the marchioness, "yes, a convent, in which I would pray for you, my mother."

"Silence! silence!" whispered Paul.

"Oh! you know him not," said Achard, whose voice was scarcely audible.

"No! but I know human nature," replied the marchioness, "he may recover a name, he! who has no name—a fortune, he! who has no fortune. And do you believe he would renounce that fortune and that name."

"Should you ask it of him, he would."

"And by what right could I demand it?" said the marchioness; "by what right could I ask him to spare me, to spare Emanuel, to spare Marguerite? He would say, 'I do not know you, madam—I have never seen you—you are my mother, and that is all I know.'"

"In his name," stammered Achard, whose tongue death was beginning to benumb, "in his name, madam, I engage, I swear—oh! my God! my God!"

The marchioness arose, observing attentively by the old

man's features, the approach of death.

"You engage, you swear!" she said, "is he here to ratify this engagement—you engage! you swear! and on your word, you would, that I should stake the years I have yet to live, against the moments which yet remain between you and death! I have entreated, I have implored, and again, I entreat and implore you to give up those papers to me."

"Those papers now are his."

"I must have them! I repeat, I must have them," continued the marchioness, gaining strength, as the dying man became more feeble.

"My God! my God! have mercy upon me!" murmured Achard.

"No one can now come," rejoined the marchioness "you told me that you wore the key of that closet always about you——"

"Would you wrest it from the hands of a dying man?"

"No," replied the marchioness, "I will wait."

"Let me die in peace," exclaimed Achard tearing the crucifix from the head of his bed, and raising it between, himself and the marchioness, he cried: "leave me! leave me; in the name of Jesus Christ!"

The marchioness fell upon her knees, bowing her head to the ground. The old man, for a moment, remained in the same awful attitude; then, by degrees, his strength forsook him, and he fell back on his bed, crossed his arms, and pressed the image of the Saviour to his breast.

The marchioness seized the lower part of the two curtains,

and without raising her head, she crossed them in such a manner as to conceal the last struggles of the dying man.

"Horror! horror!" murmured Marguerite.

"Let us kneel, and pray," said Paul.

A moment of solemn and dreadful silence then ensued, which was only interrupted by the last gasps of the dying man; these gasps became fainter by degrees, and then ceased altogether. All was over; the old man was dead.

The marchioness slowly raised her head, listened with intense anxiety for some minutes, and then, without opening the curtains, passed her hand between them, and after some effort, withdrew her hand again—she had obtained the key. She then silently arose, and with her face still turned toward the bed, walked to the closet. But at the moment she was about to unlock it, Paul, who was observing all her movements, rushed into the room, and seizing her by the arm, said—?

"Give me that key, my mother! for the marquis is dead, and those papers now belong to me."

"Justice of heaven!" exclaimed the marchioness, starting back with terror, and falling into a chair, "justice of heaven! it is my son!"

"Merciful heaven!" murmured Marguerite, throwing herself upon her knees in the outer room: "merciful heaven! he is my brother!"

Paul opened the closet, and took the casket which contained the papers.

CHAPTER XVI.—RECRIMINATION.

Thou canst save me,
Thou ought'st! thou must!
I tell thee at his feet
I'll fall a corse, ere mount his bridal bed!
Go choose betwixt my rescue and my grave.
Knowles.—The hunchbach

Notwithstanding the dreadful nature of the events which had occurred during that fatal night, Paul had not forgotten the mortal defiance which had been exchanged between himself and Lectoure. As that young gentleman would probably not know where to find him, he thought it only decorous to save Lectoure the trouble of seeking for him, and about seven in the morning, Lieutenant Walter presented himself at the castle, being charged on behalf of Paul to arrange the terms of the combat. He found Emanuel in Lectoure's apartment. The latter, on perceiving the officer, withdrew, and went down into the park, that the two young men might more freely discuss the matter. Walter had received from his commander directions to accede to every thing that might be proposed. The preliminary terms were, therefore, very speedily arranged; and it was agreed between them, that the meeting should take place in the afternoon, at four o'clock. The place of rendezvous the sea-side, near the fisherman's hut, which was about half-way between Port Louis and Auray castle. As to the weapons, they were to bring their pistols and their swords; it would be decided on the spot which they were to use, it being clearly understood that Lectoure, having been the party insulted, should have the right to make his choice.

As to the marchioness, although in the first instance petrified by the unexpected appearance of Paul, she soon recovered all her natural firmness, and drawing her veil over her face, she withdrew from the chamber, and walked across the outer room which had remained in darkness. She did not, therefore, perceive Marguerite, who was kneeling in one corner of it, mute from astonishment and terror. She after that crossed the park, entered the castle, and repaired to the room in which the scene of the contract had taken place. There, by the dying light of the wax tapers, with both her elbows resting on the table, her head supported on her hands, her eyes riveted to the paper to which Lectoure had already affixed his name, and the marquis had signed the half of his, she passed the remainder of the night reflecting upon a new determination. Thus she awaited the coming day without even thinking of taking the least repose, so powerfully did her soul of adamant support the body in which it was enclosed. This resolution was to get Emanuel and Marguerite away from the castle as speedily as possible, for it was from her children, most especially, that she desired to conceal that which was about to take place between Paul and herself.

Marguerite, who had been thus most unexpectedly present at the death-bed of the marquis and of Achard, through which she had so providentially discovered her mother's secret, rushed into Paul's arms immediately after her mother's departure from the cottage, exclaiming:

"Oh! now you are really my brother."

Her tears choked further utterance, and it was some minutes before Paul could tranquillize her agitated spirit, torn by so many and such conflicting emotions. Paul then fearing that the marchioness might enquire for her daughter, on her arrival at the castle, urged Marguerite to hasten thither; and seeing she was still trembling at the recollection of the many horrors she had witnessed, led her out of the cottage, of which he locked the door, and accompanied her to within a few paces of the castle. During this walk, Marguerite had in a certain degree, recovered her composure. Paul stood gazing at her till he saw that she had safely entered the court yard, and then returned to watch and pray beside the body of his father's faithful servant.

At seven o'clock, the marchioness hearing the noise occasioned by Lieutenant Walter's arrival at the castle, reached a bell which was standing on the table and rang it. A servant presented himself at the door in the grand livery he had worn the previous evening—it was easy to perceive that he also had not been in bed.

"Inform Mademoiselle d'Auray, that her mother is waiting for her in the drawing room," said the marchioness.

The servant obeyed, and the marchioness resumed, gloomy and motionless, her previous attitude. In a few minutes afterward, she heard a slight noise behind her, and turned round. It was Marguerite. The young girl, with more respect, perhaps, than she had ever before evinced, held out her hand toward her mother, that she might give her her hand to kiss. But the marchioness remained motionless, as if she had not understood the intention of her daughter. Marguerite let fall her hand, and silently awaited her mother's pleasure. She also wore the same dress as the night before. Sleep had hovered over the whole world, but had forgotten the inhabitants of Auray castle.

"Come nearer," said the marchioness.

Marguerite advanced one step.

"Why is it that you are thus pale and trembling," continued the marchioness.

"Madam," murmured Marguerite.

"Speak," said the marchioness.

"The death of my father—so sudden—so unexpected," stammered Marguerite; "indeed I have suffered so much this night."

"Yes, yes," rejoined the marchioness, in a hollow tone, but fixing on her daughter looks which were not altogether void of affection: "yes, the young tree bends before the wind, and is stripped of its leaves. The old oak alone withstands every tempest. I, also, have suffered, Marguerite, and suffered much. I have passed a dreadful night, and yet you see me calm and firm."

"God has endowed you with a soul, my mother, firm and austere; but you should not expect the same strength and firmness in the souls of others. You would destroy them."

"And therefore is it," replied the marchioness, letting her

hand fall upon the table, "that all I ask of you is obedience. The marquis is dead, Marguerite, and Emanuel is now the head of the family. You must immediately set out for Bennes with Emanuel."

"I!" exclaimed Marguerite, "I set out for Bennes! and for what purpose?"

"Because the chapel of the castle is too narrow to contain at the same moment the wedding party of the daughter, and the funeral procession of the father."

"My mother!" replied Marguerite with an indescribable accent of anguish, "it would seem to me to be more pious to place a longer interval between two ceremonies of so opposite a nature."

"True piety," rejoined the marchioness, "should lead us to fulfil the last wishes of the dead. Cast your eyes upon this contract, and see the first letters of your father's name."

"Oh! madam!" cried Marguerite, "allow me to ask you whether my father, when he traced these letters, which death prevented him from finishing, was in possession of his faculties, and did he write them of his own free will?"

"Of that, I am ignorant, mademoiselle," replied the marchioness, with that imperative and icy tone, which until this time had subjected all that approached her.

"I am ignorant of that, but this I know, that the influence which made him thus act, he fully understood; and I know, also, that parents, as long as they exist, should, in the eyes of their children, have the authority of God. Now, God has ordained me to effect things terrible in themselves, and I have obeyed. Do as I have done, mademoiselle, obey!"

"Madam," said Marguerite, who had remained standing, but who now seemed motionless, with somewhat of that determined tone, which in her mother was so terrible, and in which she had inherited from her; "madam! it is only three days ago, that with tearful eyes, I threw myself first at the feet of Emanuel, then at the feet of the man whom you would compel me to receive as my husband, and then at my father's. Neither of them would or could listen to me, for grasping ambition, or reckless madness hardened their hearts, and drowned my voice. At length, I am now at your feet, my mother, you are the last whom I can supplicate, but also, you are best capable of understanding me, Listen, then, attentively, to what I am about to say. Had I only to sacrifice my own happiness to your will, I would make that sacrifice: my love! I would sacrifice that also; but I must also sacrifice my son.—You are a mother, and I also, madam."

"A mother!—a mother!" cried the marchioness.

"Yes! a mother, but by a dreadful fault——"

"Be that as it may, madam, still I am a mother, and the feelings of a mother need not be sanctified, in order to be holy. Well, then, madam, tell me—for you should better comprehend these things than I—tell me if those who have given us birth, have received from heaven a voice which speaks to our hearts—have not those to whom we have given birth a voice as powerful, and when these two voices are opposed to each other, to which ought we to obey?"

"You will never hear the voice of your child." said the

marchioness; "for you will never again see him."

"I shall never again see my son!" exclaimed Marguerite, "and who, madam, can assert that positively?"

"He will himself be ignorant as to whose son he is."

"And should he some day discover it?" replied Marguerite; whose respect as a daughter was giving way before her mother's harshness; "if he should then come to me and demand an account of his birth—and this may happen, madam,"—she took up the pen—"and, with such an alternative awaiting me, tell me, ought I to sign this contract?"

"Sign it," said the marchioness.

"But," observed Marguerite, placing her trembling and convulsed fingers upon the contract, "should my husband some day discover the existence of this child; should he demand an explanation from my lover, of the wrong committed against his name and honor? If in a desperate duel, alone and without seconds—a duel in which it is agreed that one must fall, he should kill that lover, and then, tormented by his conscience, pursued by a voice from the tomb, my husband should at length become deprived of reason—"

"Be silent!" cried the marchioness, her features quivering with terror, but still doubting whether it was chance, or some unheard of discovery which dictated the words her daughter had employed: "be silent!"

"You would have me, then," continued Marguerite, who had now said too much to pause, "you would have me, then, in order to preserve my name, and that of my other children, pure and unsullied, that I should immure myself with a man deprived of reason! you would have me banish from my sight, and from his, every living being, and that I should render my heart iron, that I may no longer feel—that my eyes should never shed a tear! You would have me, then, clothe myself in mourning as a widow, before my husband's death? You would have my hair turn white, twenty years before the accustomed time?"

"Be silent! say not another word!" cried the marchioness, in a tone which proved that menaces were giving way to fear: "be silent!"

"You would have me, then," continued Marguerite, carried away by the bitterness of her grief; "you would have me, then, in order that the dreadful secret might die with those who have the keeping of it, that I should banish from their death-beds, both priest and physician—you would, in fine, that I should wander from one death-bed to another, that I might close, not the eyes, but the mouths of the dying."

"Be silent! in the name of heaven! be silent!" again cried the marchioness, wringing her hands.

"Well, then," continued Marguerite, "tell me again, my mother, to sign this paper, and all this will happen, and the malediction of the Lord will be accomplished, and the faults of the fathers shall be visited upon the children, even to the third and fourth generations."

"Ah! my God! my God!" exclaimed the marchioness, bursting into tears, "am I not sufficiently humbled—am I not sufficiently punished?"

"Pardon! pardon! madam," cried Marguerite, recalled to

filial feeling by the first tears she had ever seen her mother shed; "I implore you to forgive me."

"Yes, pardon! ask for forgiveness, unnatural daughter," said the marchioness, advancing toward Marguerite, "you who have wrenched the scourge from the hands of eternal vengeance, and have yourself applied the lash even on your mother's forehead."

"Mercy! mercy!" reiterated Marguerite; "pardon me, my mother. I knew not what I said. You had deprived me of reason—-I was mad!"

"Oh! my God! my God," said the marchioness, raising both her hands above her daughter's head, "Thou hast heard the words which have issued from my daughter's lips. It would be too much to hope that thy mercy will forget them; but at the moment thou shalt punish her, remember that I have not cursed her!"

She then moved toward the door; her daughter endeavored to retain her, but the marchioness turned toward her with an expression of countenance so fearful, that without needing to lay a command upon her, Marguerite dropped the skirt of her mother's dress, and remained with arms outstretched towards her, mute and palpitating, until the marchioness had disappeared. And when she no longer saw her, she threw herself upon the ground with so piercing a shriek, that it might have been deemed that the heart which had so much suffered, had at length broken.

CHAPTER XVII.—THE BROTHERS

Be angry as
You will, it shall have scope;
Ah, Cassius, you are yoked with a lamb
That carries anger, as the flint bears fire—
Who, much enforced, shows a hasty spark,
And straight is cold again.
And from henceforth
When you are over earnest with your brother,
He'll think your mother chides, and leave you so.

—*Shakespeare*

Our readers will perhaps have been surprised, that after the violent manner in which Paul had insulted Lectoure the day before, a meeting had not been appointed for the following morning; but Lieutenant Walter, who had been commissioned to regulate the conditions of the duel, together with Count d'Auray, had received from his commander directions to make every concession, saving on one point, and this was, that Paul would not meet Lectoure until the afternoon.

The reason for this was, that the young captain felt, that until the time arrived when he should have wound up this strange drama, in which, having in the first instance mingled only as a stranger, he at last found himself in the position of the head of the family, his life belonged not to himself, and that he had not the right to risk it. Moreover, as we

197

have seen, the delay he had fixed was not a long one; and Lectoure, who was ignorant of the reason which could have induced his adversary to require it, had acceded to it without much difficulty.

Paul had therefore determined not to lose a moment, and therefore, as soon as the hour arrived at which he could, with propriety, present himself to the marchioness, he bent his steps towards the castle.

The events of the previous evening, and of that day also, had occasioned so much confusion in the stately residence, that he entered it without meeting a single servant to announce him. He nevertheless traversed the apartments, following the direction he had before twice taken, and on going into the drawing-room, found Marguerite lying fainting on the floor.

On seeing the contract lying on the table, and his sister deprived of consciousness, Paul readily imagined that a dreadful scene must have taken place between the marchioness and her daughter. He ran to Marguerite, raised her in his arms, and opened one of the windows to give her air. The state in which Marguerite then was, proceeded more from a complete prostration of strength, than an actual fainting fit; and therefore, as soon as she felt that assistance was being rendered her, and with a kindness, which left no doubt as to the feelings of the person who had thus endeavored to relieve her, she opened her eyes, and recognized her brother, that living Providence, whom God had sent to sustain her every time she felt she was about to succumb.

Marguerite related to Paul, that her mother had endeavored to compel her to sign the contract, in order to get her to leave the castle with her brother, and that having been overcome by her grief, and carried away by the dreadful situation in which she was placed, she had allowed her mother to perceive that she knew all.

Paul comprehended at once the feelings which must have rent the heart of the marchioness, who, after twenty years of silence, isolation and anguish, saw, without being able to divine the manner in which it had been brought about, that in one moment her secret had been revealed to one of the two persons, from whom she was most anxious to conceal it. Therefore, compassionating the sufferings of his mother, he resolved to terminate them as speedily as he could, by hastening on the interview he had come to seek, and which would at once enlighten her as to the intentions of that son, whose existence she was so unwilling to acknowledge, Marguerite, on her side, wished to obtain her mother's forgiveness; she, therefore, undertook to inform the marchioness that the young captain waited her orders.

Paul, therefore, remained alone, leaning against the high chimney-piece, above which was carved the escutcheon of his family, and began to lose himself in the thoughts, which the successive and hurried events of the last few hours gave rise to, and which had rendered him the sovereign arbiter of all that house, when one of the side doors suddenly opened, and Emanuel appeared with a case of pistols in his hand. On hearing the door open, Paul turned his eyes toward them, and immediately perceiving the young man, bowed to him with that sweet and fraternal expression, which reflected in his features the serenity of his soul.

Emanuel, on the contrary, although he returned the salutation, as politeness required, allowed those hostile feelings which the presence of the man whom he regarded as his personal and determined enemy had awakened to flush his features, and they instantly assumed a look of fierce defiance.

"I was on the point of setting out to seek for you, sir," said Emanuel, placing the pistols upon the table, and remaining at some distance from Paul; "and that, however, without precisely knowing where to find you; for, like the evil genii of our popular traditions, you appear to have the gift of being every where, and nowhere. But a servant informed me that he had seen you enter the castle, and I thank you for having saved me the trouble I was about to take, in thus anticipating my desire."

"I am happy," replied Paul, "that my desire in this instance, although probably emanating from a totally different cause, has so harmoniously chimed in with yours. Well, then, I am here—what do you ask of me?"

"Cannot you divine even that, sir?" replied Emanuel, with increasing agitation. "In that case—and you will allow me to express my astonishment that it should be so—you are but ill-informed as to the duties of a gentleman and an officer, and this is a fresh insult that you put upon me."

"Believe me, Emanuel," rejoined Paul, in a calm tone—

"I yesterday called myself the count; to-day I call myself the Marquis d'Auray," said Emanuel, interrupting him with a gesture of haughtiness and contempt; "and I beg, sir, that you will not forget it."

An almost imperceptible smile passed over the lips of Paul.

"I was saying, then," continued Emanuel, "that you but imperfectly comprehend the feelings of a gentleman, if you believed that I would permit another to take up, on my behalf, a quarrel which you came here to seek. Yes, sir, for it is you who have thrown yourself across my path, and not I who have sought you."

"His lordship, the Marquis d'Auray," said Paul, smiling, "forgets his visit on board the Indienne."

"A truce to your cavils, sir, and let us at once proceed to facts. Yesterday, I know not from what strange and inexplicable feeling, when I proposed to you that, which I will not say every gentleman, every officer, but simply, any man of courage would instantly, and without hesitation, have acceded to, you refused, sir, and evading my provocation, you went, as it were, behind my back to seek an adversary, who, although not precisely a stranger to the quarrel, yet good taste should have dictated that he ought not to have been drawn into it."

"Believe me, that in this, sir," replied Paul, with the calmness and the same candor of manner which had accompanied all he said; I was compelled to yield to the exigency of the case, which did not leave me the choice of an adversary. You had proposed a duel, which I could not accept, you being my adversary, but which was perfectly indifferent to me with any other person. I am too much habituated to encounters of this description, and to encounters of a far more murderous and mortal nature, to consider an event of this kind, but as one of the usual accidents of my adventurous life. You will, however, please to remember that it was not I who sought this duel; you, yesterday, proposed it to me; but, as I could not, I again repeat it, appear as your antagonist, I selected M. de Lectoure, as I would have done M. de Nozay or M. la Jarry, because he happened to be there, within my reach—and because, if it were absolutely necessary that I should kill some one, I preferred killing an useless and insolent fop, rather than a good and honest country gentleman, who would consider himself dishonored, did he but dream that he had entered into a bargain of so vile and despicable a nature as that which the Baron de Lectoure has, in reality, proposed to you."

"'Tis well, sir," said Emanuel, jeeringly; "continue to constitute yourself as the redresser of wrongs, to dub yourself the knight-errant of oppressed princesses, and to shield yourself under the buckler of your mysterious replies! As long as this antiquated quixotism does not come in collision with my views, my interests, and my engagements, I will fully permit it to wander over the whole earth, and ocean also, even from pole to pole, and I shall merely smile at it as it passes by me; but whenever this madness breaks out against me, as yours has done, sir; whenever, in the intimate concerns of a family of which I am the head, I meet a stranger, who orders as a master where I alone have the right to raise my voice, I shall present myself before him, as I now do before you, should I have the happiness to meet him alone as I do you, and then feeling assured, that no one will come to interrupt us before I had obtained the necessary explanation, I would say to him: 'You have, if not insulted me, at all events wounded my feelings, sir, by coming to my house, and injuring me in my in-terests, and my family affections. It is then with me, and not with another, that you ought to fight, and you shall fight with me.'"

"You are mistaken, Emanuel," replied Paul; "I will not fight, at all events, with you; the thing is impossible."

"Oh! sir, the time of enigmas is gone by," cried Emanuel, impatiently; "we live in the midst of a world, in which at every moment we elbow a reality. Let us, therefore, leave the poetical and the mysterious, to the authors of romances and tragedies. Your presence in this castle has been marked by circumstances too fatal to render it necessary to add that which is not, to that which is. Lusignan returned, notwithstanding the order which condemned him to transportation; my sister, who, for the first time, has shown herself rebellious against the orders of her mother; my father, killed by your mere presence: these are the disasters by which you have been accompanied, which have heralded you from another hemisphere, and have formed your funereal escort: for all this, you have to account to me; therefore, speak, sir; speak as a man should to a man, in the broad daylight, face to face, and not as a phantom gliding in the darkness, which escapes under the cloud of night, letting fall some few solemn and prophetic words, as if from the other world. Such things are well calculated to terrify nurses and children! Speak, sir, speak! Look at me, you will see that I am calm. If you have anything to reveal to me I will listen to you."

"The secret which you ask of me is not my own," replied Paul, whose perfect calmness strongly contrasted with the feverish excitement of Emanuel; "believe what I have said, and do not insist farther. Farewell!"

After pronouncing these words, Paul moved toward the door.

"Oh!" cried Emanuel, rushing between him and the door, to prevent his passage; "you shall not leave me thus, sir! I have you now, we are alone in this room, without fear of any interruption, into which, it was not I that enticed you, but you have come here of your own free will. Therefore, hearken to that which I am about to say. The person you have insulted is myself! the person to whom you owe satisfaction is myself!

"The person with whom you have to fight is——"

"You are mad, sir," tranquilly replied Paul; "I have already told you it is impossible. Therefore, allow me to withdraw."

"Take care, sir," cried Emanuel, stretching out his hand to the box, and taking out the pistols; "take care, sir. After having done every thing in my power to compel you to act as a gentleman, I may treat you as a brigand.—You are here in a house, in which you are a total stranger; you have entered it, I know not how, nor for what purpose; if you have not come into it to despoil us of our gold and jewels, you have entered it to steal the obedience of a daughter to her mother, and to cancel the sacred promise given by a friend to a friend. In one case or the other, you are a violator, whom I have met at the moment that his hands were about to seize a treasure; that treasure, is honor, the most precious of all riches! Come, sir, believe me, you will do better to accept this weapon"—Emanuel endeavored to thrust one of the pistols into Paul's hand—"and defend yourself."

"You may kill me, sir," replied Paul, again placing his elbow on the chimney-piece, as if he were continuing an ordinary conversation; "although I do not believe that God would permit so great a crime: but you shall not force me to fight with you. I have before told you so, and I repeat it."

"Take the pistol, sir!" cried Emanuel, "take it, sir, I tell you! you believe that the threat I am making is but a vain menace; undeceive yourself! for three days have you fatigued my patience! for three days have you filled my soul with gall and hatred! for three days have I familiarised my mind with the idea of ridding myself of you; whether it be by a duel or by murder! Do not imagine, that the dread of punishment withholds my hand; this castle is isolated, mute, and deaf. The sea is there; and before you could be even laid in the tomb, I should be in England. Therefore, sir, for the last time, I say to you, take this pistol and defend yourself." Paul, without uttering a word, gently put the pistol aside.

"Well then!" cried Emanuel, exasperated to the highest degree, by the sangfroid of his adversary; "as you will not defend yourself like a man, die like a dog!" And so saying, he raised the muzzle of the pistol to the level of the captain's breast.

At that moment a dreadful shriek was heard; it was Marguerite, who had returned from her mother, and who had, at a glance, comprehended all that had happened. She rushed upon Emanuel, and at that instant he fired the pistol, but the direction of the ball having been changed by the young girl's striking up his arm, it passed two or three inches above Paul's head, and shattered the glass above the chimney-piece.

"My brother!" cried Marguerite, with one bound, springing to were Paul stood, and throwing her arms around him: "my brother, are you not wounded?"

"Your brother!" exclaimed Emanuel, letting fall the pistol which was still smoking; "your brother!"

"Well, Emanuel!" said Paul, with the same calmness which he had evinced during the whole of this painful scene; "do you now comprehend why it was I could not fight with you?"

At that moment, the marchioness appeared at the door, pale as a spectre, for she had heard the report of the pistol; then looking around her with an expression of infinite terror, and seeing that no one was wounded, she silently raised her eyes to heaven, as if to ask if its anger was at length appeased. She remained thus for some time in an attitude of mental thanksgiving. When she again cast down her eyes, Emanuel and Marguerite were on their knees before her, each holding one of her hands, and covering it with tears and kisses.

"I thank you, my children," said the marchioness, after a short silence; "and now leave me with this young man."

Marguerite and Emanuel bowed with an expression of the most profound respect, and obeyed the command of their mother.

CHAPTER XVIII—RECOGNITION.

Oh! my mother!
You do not know the heart that you have pierced!
I—I—thy son—thine Arthur—I avenge?
Never on thee.

Live happy—love my brother—
Forget that I was born.
Here, here—these proofs—
These—these!

Oh! see you where the words are blistered
With my hot tears?
I wept—it was for joy—
I did not think of lands, of name, of birthright—
I did but think these arms should clasp a' mother.

Bulwer.—The Sea Captain.

The marchioness closed the door as soon as they had withdrawn, advanced into the middle of the room, and went without looking at Paul, and leaning upon the arm-chair in which the marquis had the night before been seated to sign the contract. There she remained standing, with her eyes cast upon the ground. Paul for a moment experienced the desire to throw himself upon his knees before her, but there was upon the features of the marchioness such an expression of severity, that he repressed the yearnings of his heart, and stood motionless awaiting her commands. After a few moments of ice-like silence, the marchioness addressed him. "You desired to see me, sir, and I have come to know your will—you wished to speak to me—I am listening."

These words were uttered without the marchioness making the least movement—her lips trembled, rather than opened—it seemed a marble statue that was speaking.

"Yes, madam," replied Paul, in a tone of intense feeling, "yes, yes, I desired to speak with you; it is long since first this desire was cherished in my heart, and it has never left me. Recollections of infancy preyed upon the mind of the grown man. I remembered a woman who would formerly glide to my cradle, and in my youthful dreams, I thought her the guardian angel of my infancy. Since that time, still so fresh in my memory, although so distant, more than once, believe me, I have awakened with a start, imagining that I had felt upon my forehead the impression of a maternal kiss: and then seeing that there was no one near me, I would call that person, hoping she would, perhaps, return. It is now twenty years since first I thus had called, and this is the first time she has replied to me. Can it have been as I have often fearfully imagined, that you would have trembled at again beholding me? Can it be true, as I at this moment fear, that you have naught to say to me?"

"And had I feared your return," said the marchioness, in a hollow tone, "should I have been to blame? You appeared before me only yesterday, sir, and now the mystery which ought to have been concealed to all but God and myself, is known to both my children."

"Is it my fault that God has been pleased to reveal the secret to them? Was it I that conducted Marguerite, despairing and in tears, to the bedside of her dying father, whose protection she had gone to ask, and whose confession she was compelled to hear? Was it I that led her to Achard, and was it not you, madam, that followed her thither? As to Emanuel, the report you heard, and that shattered glass, attest, that I would have preferred death rather than to have saved my life at the expense of your secret. No, no, believe me, madam, I am the instrument, and not the hand; the effect, and not the cause. No, madam, it is God who has brought about all this, that you might see at your feet, as you have just now seen them, your two children whom you have so long banished from your arms!"

"But there is a third," said the marchioness, in a voice in which emotion began to evince itself, "and I know not what I have to expect from him."

"Let me accomplish a last duty, madam, and that once fulfilled, he will on his knees await your orders."

"And of what nature is this duty?"

"It is to restore his brother to the rank to which he is entitled, his sister to that happiness which she has lost—to his mother that tranquillity of mind, which she has so long sought in vain."

"And yet, thanks to you," replied the marchioness, "M. de Maurepas refused to M. de Lectoure the regiment he had solicited for my son."

"Because," replied Paul, taking the commission from his pocket and laying it on the table, "because the king had already granted it to me, for the brother of Marguerite."

The marchioness cast her eyes upon the commission, and saw that it was made out in the name of Emanuel d'Auray.

"And yet you would give the hand of Marguerite to a man without name, without fortune—and what is more, to a man who is banished."

"You are mistaken, madam; I would give Marguerite to the man she loves. I would give Marguerite not to the banished Lusignan, but to the Baron Anatole de Lusignan, his majesty's governor of the Island of Gaudaloupe—there is his commission also." The marchioness looked at the parchment, and saw that in this instance, as in the former one, Paul had uttered but the truth.

"Yes, I acknowledge it," she replied, "these will satisfy the ambition of Emanuel, and confer happiness on Marguerite."

"And at the same time, secures your tranquillity madam; for Emanuel will join his regiment, and Marguerite will follow her husband. You will then remain here alone, as you have, alas! so frequently desired."

The marchioness sighed.

"Is not this all you desire, or have I deceived myself," continued Paul.

"But," said the marchioness, "how can I recall the promise given to the Baron de Lectoure?"

"The marquis is dead, madam," replied Paul; "is not the death of a husband and a father a sufficient cause for the adjournment of a marriage?"

The marchioness, without replying, seated herself in the arm-chair, took a pen and paper, wrote a few lines, folded the letter, and putting on the address the name of the Baron de Lectoure, she rang the bell for the servant. After waiting a few moments, during which time, both Paul and herself remained silent, a servant came into the room.

"In two hours from this time, you will deliver this to the Baron de Lectoure," said the Marchioness. The servant took the letter and withdrew.

"And now," continued the marchioness, looking at Paul, "now sir, that you have done justice to the innocent, it remains to you to pardon the guilty. You have papers which prove your birth, you are the elder—at all events, in the eyes of the law. The fortunes of Emanuel and Marguerite are yours by right. What do you require in exchange for these papers?"

Paul took them from his pocket, and showing them to the marchioness, said, "Here are the documents, look at them— they are the letters you wrote to my poor father—look here, they are moistened by my tears, for I read them last night, while watching by Achard's corpse." Then approaching the fire-place, he held them over the flaming wood, saying, "permit me even but once to call you mother! call me but once your son, and——"

"Can it be possible!" exclaimed the marchioness, rising.

"You speak of name, of fortune," continued Paul, with an expression of profound melancholy; "what need have I of them. I have by my own sword gained a rank which few men of my age have ever attained—I have acquired a name which is pronounced with blessings by one nation, andi with terror by another. I could, did it so please me, amass a fortune, worthy of being bequeathed to a king. What, then, are your name your fortune, and your rank, to me, if you have nothing else to offer me—if you do not give me that which I have incessantly, and in every position of my life most yearned for—that which I have not the power to create—which God had granted to me, but which misfortune wrested from me— that which you alone can restore to me—a mother!"

"My son!" exclaimed the marchioness, overcome at length, by his tears, and supplicating accent, "my son! my son! my son!"

"Ah!" exclaimed Paul, letting the papers fall into the flames, which speedily consumed them, "ah! that missed appellation has at length escaped your lips—that tender name so long desired, and which I have so unceasingly prayed to hear addressed to me. Merciful heaven! I thank thee."

The marchioness had fallen back into her chair, and Paul had thrown himself upon his knees, his head leaning upon her bosom. At length the marchioness gently raised him.

"Look at me!" she said; "for twenty years, this is the first tear that has ever escaped my eyelids, give me your hand!"— she placed it upon her heart—"for twenty years this is the first feeling of happiness with which my heart has palpitated. Come to my arms! For twenty years this is the first caress I have either given or received. These twenty years have doubtless been my expiation, since God now pardons me, for he has restored to me the power of weeping, of feeling joy, and has permitted me to embrace my son. Thanks to G-od! and thanks to thee, my son!"

"My mother!" cried Paul, "my beloved mother!"

"And I trembled at the thoughts of seeing you again—I trembled when I did see you—I knew not—I could not have imagined that such feelings still existed in my heart. Oh! I bless thee! I bless thee!"

At that moment, the tolling of the chapel bell was heard: the marchioness shuddered. The funeral hour had arrived. The bodies of the noble Marquis d'Auray and that of the poor man Achard, were about to be returned to earth at the same moment.

"This hour must be consecrated to prayer," said the marchioness: "I must now leave you."

"I must sail to-morrow, my mother," said Paul; "shall I not once more see you?"

"Oh! yes, yes," replied the marchioness, "we must meet again."

"Well, then, my mother, this evening I shall be at the park gate. There is a spot which is sacred to me, and to which I must pay a last visit. I shall expect to meet you there. It is on that spot, my mother, that we should say farewell."

"I will be there," said the marchioness.

"Here, my mother, here," said Paul, "take these commissions: the one for Emanuel, and the other for the husband of Marguerite. Let the happiness of your children be conferred by yourself. Believe me, mother, you have bestowed more on me than I on them."

The marchioness retired to shut herself up in her oratory. Paul left the castle, and proceeded toward the hut of the fisherman.

CHAPTER XIX.—THE FAREWELL.

Hark! she has bless'd her son—I bid ye witness,
Ye listening heavens—thou circumambient air;
The ocean sighs it back—and with the murmur
Bustle the happy leaves.

All nature breathes
Aloud—-aloft—to the Great Parent's ear,
The blessing of the mother on her child.

ON approaching the fisherman's hut, the place appointed with Lectoure, Paul perceived Lusignan and Walter, who were waiting for him.

Precisely at the hour agreed, Lectoure appeared on horseback; he had been obliged to find his way as he best could, for he had no guide, and his own servant was as much a stranger as himself in that part of the country. On seeing him at a distance the young men came out of the hut. The baron instantly put his horse into a gallop, to hasten to them. When within a few paces of them he alighted from his horse, and threw the rein to his servant.

"I trust you will pardon me, gentlemen," said he, "that I should have approached you thus alone, like a forsaken orphan; but the hour selected by that gentleman," he added, raising his hat to Paul, who returned the salutation, "was precisely that fixed upon for the funeral obsequies of the marquis; I have therefore left Emanuel to fulfil the duties of a son, and have come here without a second, trusting that I had to deal with an adversary generous enough to procure some friend of his own to aid me in this dilemma."

"We are entirely at your service, baron," replied Paul; "here are two friends of mine. Select which you please, and he who shall be honored by your choice, will instantly become yours."

"I have no preference, I swear to you," said Lectoure; "please to designate which of these two gentlemen you may desire should reader me this service."

"Walter," said Paul, "be so good as to officiate as second to the baron."

The lieutenant assented; the two adversaries again bowed to each other.

"And now, sir," continued Paul, "permit me, before our respective seconds, to address a few words to you, not of apology, but explanation."

"At your own pleasure, sir, replied Lectoure.

"When I uttered the words which have been the cause of your coming hither, the events which have since occurred at the castle were hidden in the womb of time, and these events might have entailed the misery of a whole family. You, sir, had on your side Madame d'Auray, Emanuel, and the Marquis—Marguerite had but me alone. Every chance was, therefore, in your favor. It was for this reason that I addressed myself directly to you, for had I fallen by your hand from circumstances which must for ever remain hidden to you,

Marguerite could not have married you. If I had killed you, the case would have been still more simplified, and requires no commentary.

"This exordium is really most logical, sir," replied the baron, smiling, and tapping his boots with his riding-whip; "let us proceed, if you please, to the main body of the discourse." |

"Now," continued Paul, bowing in sign of acquiescence, "every circumstance has changed; the marquis is dead, Emanuel has received his commission, the marchioness renounces your alliance, honorable as it may be, and Marguerite marries the Baron Anatole de Lusignan, who, for that reason, I did not name your second."

"Ah! ah!" exclaimed Lectoure, "then that is the true meaning of the note which a servant delivered to me at the moment I was about to leave the castle. I had the simplicity to imagine that it was merely an adjournment. It appears that it was a dismissal in due form. 'Tis well, sir, and now to the peroration."

"It will be as simple and frank as the explanation, sir. I did not know you—I had no desire to know you; chance threw us in presence of each other, and with opposing interests—hence our collision. Then, as I have before told you, mistrusting fate, I wished in some measure to make sure of a result. But now affairs have become so altered that either my death or yours would be altogether useless, and would merely add bloodshed to the winding up of this drama; and tell me candidly, sir, do you thank it would be worth while to risk our lives to so little purpose?"

"I might, perhaps, agree with you in opinion, sir, had I not performed so long a journey," replied Lectoure: "Not having the honor to espouse Mademoiselle Marguerite d'Auray, I should desire, at least, to have the honor of crossing swords with you. It shall not be said that I have travelled all the way from Paris into Brittany for nothing. I am at your orders, sir," continued Lectoure, drawing his sword, and with it saluting his adversary.

"At your good pleasure, sir," replied Paul, and replying to the salutation in the same manner.

The two young men then advanced towards each other— their swords crossed—at the third parry Lectoure's sword was twisted from his hand, and flew to a distance of twenty yards.

"Before taking sword in hand," said Paul, "I had offered an explanation, and now, sir, I trust you will be pleased to accept my apology."

"And this time I will accept it, sir," said Lectoure, in the same careless and easy manner, as if nothing particular had occurred. "Pick up my sword, Dick."

His servant ran to fetch it, handed it to his master, who very tranquilly put it into the scabbard.

"Now," continued he, "if either of you, gentlemen, have any orders for Paris, I am about to return there, and from this spot."

"Tell the king, sir," replied Paul, bowing, and in his turn sheathing his sword, "that I feel happy that the sword he gave me to be employed against the English, has remained unstained by the blood of one of my own countrymen."

And then the two young men again bowed to each other. Lectoure remounted his horse, and at about a hundred paces from the sea shore, got into the high road leading to Vannes, and galloped off; while his servant went to the castle to get his travelling carriage, with which Lectoure had ordered him to rejoin him speedily.

"And now, Mr. Walter," said Paul, "you must send the long-boat to the nearest creek to Auray castle, and have every thing in readiness to set sail tonight."

The lieutenant immediately set out for Port Louis, and Paul and Lusignan returned into the fisherman's hut.

During this time Emanuel and Marguerite had fulfilled the mournful duty to which they had been summoned by the chapel bell. The body of the marquis had been deposited in the emblazoned tomb of his ancestors, and Achard's in the humble cemetery outside the chapel, and then the brother and sister repaired to their mother's apartment. The marchioness delivered to Emanuel the commission which he so anxiously coveted, and gave to Marguerite her unexpected consent to her marriage with Lusignan. She then handed to Marguerite the king's sign manual appointing Lusignan governor of Guadaloupe. And then, in order that the emotions which they experienced should not be renewed, and which were the more poignant, because they were concealed within their own breasts, for neither of them made any allusion to past events, the mother and the children embraced each other for the last time, each feeling the innate conviction that they should never meet again.

The remainder of the day was occupied in the necessary preparations for departure. Toward the evening the marchioness left the castle, to meet Paul at the place which he had appointed. When passing through the court-yard she perceived a carriage, with horses already attached to it, standing on one side of it, and the young midshipman, Arthur, with four sailors, on the other. Her heart was oppressed by the sight of this two-fold preparation. She, however, passed on, and went into the park, without giving way to her emotions, so much had her long-continued restraint upon natural feelings given her the power of self-command.

However, when she had reached a small clearing, from which she could see Achard's house, she paused, for her knees trembled beneath her, and she was obliged to lean for support against a tree, while she pressed her hand to her breast to restrain the violent beatings of her heart. For there are souls which present danger, however imminent, cannot cause to quail, but which tremble at the remembrance of perils past; and the marchioness recalled to mind the agonizing fears and emotions to which she had been for twenty years a prey, and during which time she had daily visited that house, now closed never again to be opened. She, however, soon overcame this weakness, and reached the park gate.

There she again paused. Above all the trees rose the summit of a gigantic oak, whose wide spreading branches could be discerned from many places in the park. Often had the eyes of the marchioness remained riveted for hours upon its verdant dome: but never had she dared to seek repose beneath its shade. It was there, however, that she had promised to meet Paul, and there Paul was awaiting her. At length she made a last effort, and entered the forest.

From a distance she perceived a man kneeling upon the ground in the attitude of prayer. She slowly approached him, and kneeling down by his side, prayed also. When the prayer was concluded, they both rose, and without uttering a word, the marchioness placed her arm around Paul's neck, and leaned her head upon his shoulder. After some moments' silence, they heard the noise of the wheels of a carriage at a distance. The marchioness shuddered, and made a sign to Paul to listen; it was Emanuel setting out to join his regiment. Shortly afterwards Paul pointed in a direction opposite to that in which they had heard the noise, and showed the marchioness a boat gliding rapidly and silently upon the surface of the ocean; it was Marguerite going on board the frigate.

The marchioness listened to the noise of the receding wheels as long as she could hear it, and followed with anxious eyes the movements of the boat, as long as she could distinguish it; then she turned toward Paul, and raising her eyes to heaven, for she felt that the moment was approaching, when he, whom she was leaning upon, would, in his turn, leave her, she exclaimed—

"May God bless, as I now bless, the duteous son, who was the last to leave his mother."

Saying these words, she threw her arms around his neck, pressed him convulsively to her heart, and kissed him; then gazing at him intently, she seemed to be scanning every outline of his face, and then, again, rapturously embraced him.

"Yes," she cried, "in every feature he is the living resemblance of my poor lost Morlaix," then for some moments she seemed to be absorbed in thought; at last after a seemingly violent struggle, she continued, "Paul, you have refused to accept any portion of that fortune to which you are legally entitled, although you know the wealth of the Auray family is unbounded—and that the fortune which I inherit in my own right, from the family of Sablé, is very large." Paul shook his head. "Well, then, there is one thing that you must receive from your mother, as her parting gift. It is twenty years since I have dared to look upon it, and yet I have clung to its possession—it is your father's portrait, presented to me when I was authorized to receive it—when, by the assent of both our families, he was to have become my husband—take it, my dear son, for although it tears my heart to part with it, yet I feel that I shall be more tranquil when it is in your possession—to no one but yourself would I have given it. You will sometimes look upon it, and you will think of your mother, who must now remain for ever isolated from the world. But it is better that it should be so—henceforward all my moments shall be spent in making my peace with Heaven."

While saying these words, she had drawn from her

pocket a case, which she put into Paul's hands, and which he had eagerly opened, and gazed with intense interest at the features of his father. The miniature was richly set in diamonds of great value.

Then summoning all her fortitude, the marchioness for the last time kissed her son, who was kneeling before her, and tearing herself from his arms, she returned alone to the castle.

The next morning the inhabitants of Port Louis vainly sought the frigate they had seen only the evening before, and which for fifteen days had remained at anchor in the outer roads of Lorient. As on the former occasion, she had disappeared without their being able to comprehend the cause of her arrival, or the motive of her so sudden departure.

EPILOGUE.

Last scene of all

That ends this strange, eventful history.

Five years had elapsed since the occurrence of the events we have related. The independence of the United States had been recognized; New York, the last strong-hold of the English, had been evacuated. The roar of cannon,-which had resounded in the Indian seas, as well as in the Gulf of Mexico, had ceased to thunder. Washington, in the solemn meeting of Congress of the 28th December, 1783, had resigned his commission as general-in-chief, and had retired to Mount Vernon, his parental estate, without any other recompence than that of being allowed to receive and send letters free of charge; and the tranquillity which America had begun to enjoy, had extended to the French colonies in the West Indies; for the mother country having espoused the American cause, they had been several times exposed to the hostile attempts of Great Britain. Among these islands, Guadaloupe had been more particularly threatened, in consequence of its military and commercial importance; but, thanks to the vigilance of its new governor, the attempts of the enemy to land there had always failed, and France had not to mourn over any serious discomfiture in this important position, so that at the commencement of the year 1784, the island, without being altogether denuded of warlike appearance, which was maintained in it more from custom than from necessity, the

225

inhabitants generally had applied themselves anew to the cultivation of the numerous products which form its riches.

If our readers will be pleased by a last effort of their complaisance, to accompany us to the other side of the Atlantic, and land with us at the port of Basseterre, we will conduct them amidst fountains which jet on every side, through the street which leads to the promenade, called Champ d'Arbaud; then, after having availed ourselves of the cool shade of the tamarind trees, planted on each side of it, till we have proceeded about two-thirds of its length, we will turn upon the left up a small beaten road, which conducts to the gate of a garden, the upper part of which commands a view of the whole town.

When we have arrived there, we will allow them for a few moments to inhale the evening breeze, so refreshingly sweet after the mid-day heat of the month of May, and they can cast a glance with us over the luxuriant vegetation of the tropics.

With our backs turned to the woody and volcanic mountains, which divide the western part of the island, and amid which arise, crowned with their plumes of smoke and sparks, the two calcined pinnacles of the sulphur mountain, we have at our feet, sheltered by the hills, which have been named Bellevue, Mont-Désir, Beau Soliel, Espérance and Saint Charles, the city gracefully descending towards the sea, the waves of which sparkling with the last rays of the setting sun, laves its white walls. The horizon, formed by the ocean, lying like a vast and limpid mirror, and to the right and left, the most beautiful and richest plantation of the island; large square fields of coffee trees, transplanted originally from Arabia, with their knotty and flexible branches, covered with dark green glossy leaves, of an oblong and pointed form, and bearing clusters of flowers as white as snow; long rows of cotton plants, covering with a rich carpet of verdure, the dry and stony soil, on which they thrive best, and among which we see, like so many colossal ants, negroes occupied in reducing to two or three, the thousand shoots which sprout out from each stalk. And then again, but in more level and well sheltered spots, in which the soil is richer and more argillaceous, we see plantations of cocoa trees, first introduced into the West Indies by the Jew, Benjamin Dacosta, with their lofty trunks and porous branches, covered with fawn colored bark, from which large oblong leaves are pending, among which we see fresh shoots of a soft rose color, which contrast strongly with the long, curved and yellow fruit, which bends the branches with its weight. And further off, whole fields of the plant, discovered at Tabaco, first brought to France by the Ambassador of Francis II., who presented it to Catherine de Medicis, from which circumstance it derived its name of Herbe-a-là-reine.* This did not, however, prevent it from being, like every popular thing, in the first instance, excommunicated and proscribed, in Europe and Asia, by the two powers who then divided the world, proscribed by the Grand Duke of Muscovy, Michael Fedorowich, by the Turkish Sultan Amurath IV., by the Emperor of Persia, and excommunicated by Pope Urban VIII. Here and there, we see springing up to a height of forty or fifty feet above all the shrubs and plants, by which it is surrounded, the banana tree of Paradise, of which, according to tradition, the oval leaves, seven or eight feet in length, served to form the first garment of the first created woman. And finally, elevated above all the rest, and standing forth pre-eminent, whether hacked by the azure of the Heavens, or by the dark green tea, the cocoa-nut and the palm-tree, those two giants of the Western Archipelago graceful and prodigal, as is everything that is powerful. Figure to yourselves, then these beautiful hills, intersected by seventy rivers, eased in beds, ninety feet in depth; these mountains illuminated during the day by a tropical sun, at night, by the volcano of the sulphur mountain; that vegetation, which never is arrested, the new leaves of which succeed the leaves which fall; this soil so salubrious, and air so pure, that notwithstanding the insensate experiments that man, the real enemy of himself, has made by transporting serpents from Martinique, and Saint Lucie, it was found that they could neither live nor reproduce there, and then judge after the sufferings they had endured in Europe, of the happiness which Antole de Lusignan and Marguerite d'Auray must have enjoyed there.

* Queen's Grass.

To a life agitated by the passions, to that struggle of natural rights against legal power, to that succession of scenes in which all earthly pains, from childbirth even to death, had played their part, had succeeded a life of pure delights, each day of which had passed on calmly and tranquilly;

the only clouds that darkened it, arose from that vague uneasiness for distant friends, which as if borne upon the air, and which contracts the heart like a painful presentiment. However, from time to time, whether by newspapers, or by vessels, touching at the island, Anatole and Marguerite had obtained some intelligence of the generous being who had so powerfully served them as a protector; they had heard of his victories; that after he had left them, he had been appointed to the command of a small squadron, and had destroyed the English establishments on the coast of Acadia, which had gained for him the title of commodore; that, in an engagement with the Serapis and the Countess of Scarborough, after a combat yard-arm to yard-arm, which lasted four hours, he had obliged the two frigates to strike to him, and that finally, as a reward for the services he had rendered to the cause of American Independence, he had received the public thanks of Congress, who had voted him a gold medal, and had selected him to command the frigate America, to which that name had been given as being the finest in the service, and the command of which had been conferred on him as the bravest of its officers; but this splendid ship had been presented by Congress to the King of France, to replace the Magnifique, which had been lost at Boston. Paul Jones, after conducting this frigate to Havre, had joined the fleet of the Count de Vaudreuil, who had projected an attack upon Jamaica. This last intelligence had overjoyed the hearts of Lusignan and Marguerite, for this enterprize would bring Paul into their latitude, and they hoped at last they should soon see their brother and their friend; but peace, as we have before said, had intervened, and from that time, they had heard no more of the adventurous seaman.

In the evening of the day on which we have transported our readers from the wild shores of Brittany to the fertile coast of Guadaloupe, the young family were assembled in the very garden which we have entered, and which commands a view of the immense panorama we have described; the foreground of which is formed by the city, at its feet the ocean, studded with islands in the distance.

Marguerite had promptly habituated herself to the soft listlessness of Creole life; and her mind now tranquil and full of happiness, she gave herself up to the dolce far niente, which renders the sensual existence of the colonies a half sleep, the incidents of which appear as dreams.

She was lying with her daughter in a Peruvian hammock, netted with the silken fibres of the aloe, and ornamented with the most brilliant colored plumes of the rarest tropical birds; her son was swinging her with a soft and regular motion, and Lusignan was holding one of her hands between both his. She was still pale, but delicate and graceful as a wild lily. Her looks were vacantly wandering over the immense extent of ocean lying before her, and she felt her soul and senses enraptured by all the bliss which heaven can promise, and all the enjoyments which this earth can offer. At that moment, and as if everything concurred to complete the magic spectacle which every evening she came there to contemplate, and which every succeeding evening she found still more marvellously beautiful, there suddenly appeared, doubling the cape Trois Pointes, and looking like an ocean king, a large vessel, gliding along the surface of the sea without more apparent effort than a swan playing upon the tranquil bosom of a lake. Marguerite was the first to perceive it, and without speaking, for every action is a fatigue under that burning clime, she made a sign with her head to Lusignan, who directed his looks to the spot she had indicated, and then, like her, silently followed with his eyes the rapid and graceful movements of the vessel. By degrees as she approached, and as the elegant and delicate proportions of her masts amidst the mass of sails which they sustained, could be discerned, which, in the first instance, had seemed a cloud floating upon the horizon—they began to discover in one corner of her flag the stars of America, equal in number to the States they represent. One same idea shot instantly through their minds, and they exchanged a glance, radiant with hope that they were, perhaps, about to receive some news of Paul. Lusignan immediately ordered a negro to bring a telescope: but before he had returned, a hope still more delightful pervaded both their hearts. It appeared to Lusignan and Marguerite that they recognized an old friend in the frigate that was approaching. To persons, however, unaccustomed, it is so difficult to distinguish, at a great distance, signs which speak at once to the eye of an experienced seaman, that they did not yet dare to have faith in this hope, and which, indeed, was more an instinctive presentiment than positive reality. At last the negro brought the so much longed for telescope. Lusignan uttered a cry of joy, and then handed it to Marguerite: he had recognized the sculpture of Guillaume Costou, upon the prow of the vessel, and it was really the Indienne which was advancing towards Basseterre.

Lusignan raised Marguerite from the hammock and placed her on her feet, for their first impulse was to hasten to the harbour; but then they reflected that Paul had left the Indienne nearly five years, at the time that his promotion entitled him to the command of a larger vessel, and that she might now be under the orders of another captain, and they paused with palpitating hearts and trembling limbs. During this time, their son Hector had taken up the telescope, and placing it to his eye, looked through it, and soon after exclaimed,—"Father, see there,—upon the deck stands an officer, dressed in a black coat, embroidered with gold, just like the one in the picture of my dear friend, Paul!" Lusignan hastily snatched the glass from his son's hands, looked through it for a few moments, then again passed it to Marguerite, who, after directing it toward the vessel, let it fall, and then they threw themselves into each other's arms; they had recognized their friend, who, as he was about to visit them, had put on the dress which we have before said he had generally worn. At this instant the frigate passed the fort, which it saluted with three guns, and the fort returned the salute with an equal number.

From the moment that Lusignan and Marguerite had acquired the certitude that their friend and brother was actually on board the Indienne, they had hastened down the mountain, followed by young Hector, towards the port, leaving their little Blanche in the hammock. The captain had also recognized them, so that at the moment they left the garden he had ordered a boat to be lowered, and, thanks to the united strength of ten vigorous oarsmen, he had rapidly glided over the distance between the anchorage ground and the port, and had sprung upon the jetty at the instant that his friends arrived there. Such sensations as then filled their breasts cannot be expressed in words; tears are their only interpreter. And thus their joy more closely resembled grief, for they all wept, even to the child, who wept because he saw them weep.

After giving some orders relating to the vessel, the young commodore, with his delighted friends, slowly ascended the hill down which they had rushed so rapidly to meet him. Paul told them that the expedition of Admiral Vaudreuil having failed, he had returned to Philadelphia, and peace having been signed, as we have before mentioned, with England, the Congress, as a token of gratitude, had presented him with the first ship he had commanded as captain.

Upon hearing this, Lusignan and Marguerite experienced the most lively joy, for they hoped that their brother had come with the intention of taking up his abode with them; but the character of the young seaman was too adventurous, and stood too much in need of excitement, to sink quietly down into the monotonous and unvaried dulness of a life on shore. He informed his friends that he had but eight days to remain with them, after which he should seek in another quarter of the globe, to follow the profession he had adopted.

These eight days passed by as rapidly as a dream, and notwithstanding the reiterated entreaties of both Lusignan and Marguerite, Paul would not consent to delay his departure even for twenty-four hours. He was still the same ardent determined being, considering the execution of a resolution he had once formed as a positive duty, and more austere with regard to himself than toward others.

The hour of separation had arrived. Marguerite and Lusignan wished to accompany the young commodore on board his ship; but Paul wished not to prolong the grief of this leave-taking. When they reached the jetty he embraced them for the last time, then jumped into his boat, which was rowed away as swiftly as an arrow. Marguerite and Lusignan followed him with their eyes until his boat had disappeared on the leeward side of the frigate, and they sorrowfully reascended the hill to watch the ship's departure, from the same terrace from which they had before discerned its arrival.

At the moment they reached it, they observed that activity and bustle on board the frigate which always precede the departure of a vessel. The sailors had surrounded the capstan, and were employed in getting up the anchor, and thanks to the pureness of the atmosphere, the sonorous and lively cries of the seamen reached the ears of Lusignan and Marguerite; the anchor was soon apeak, and they saw it rising slowly under the ship's bows; then the sails dropped successively from the yards, from the royals to the courses, and the ship, seemingly endowed with an instinctive and animated feeling, gracefully turned her prow toward the harbour's mouth, and beginning to move, cut through the waves with an easy motion, as if merely gliding upon their surface. Then, as if the frigate might be abandoned to her own will, they saw the young commodore spring upon the stern rails, and devote all his attention to the land he was thus leaving. Lusignan took out his handkerchief and made a signal, to which Paul replied. And then, when they could no longer perceive each other with the naked eye, they had recourse to their telescopes, and, thanks to this ingenious invention, they retarded the separation for another hour. They all felt a presentiment that this separation would be eternal.

The vessel gradually diminished upon the horizon, and darkness was about to cover the heavens, when Lusignan ordered a quantity of wood to be brought upon the terrace, to form a beacon fire, which was instantly ignited, in order that Paul, whose vessel was nearly enshrouded in the darkness, might continue to fix his eyes upon that spot until he had doubled Cape Trois Pointes. Lusignan and Marguerite had for an hour lost sight of the ship, while Paul, thanks to their large brilliant fire, might still perceive them, when a bright flame, like to a flash of lightning, appeared on the horizon, and in a few seconds the report of a gun, similar to the prolonged sound of distant thunder, reached their ears, and all again was silent. Lusignan and Marguerite had received Paul's last farewell.

And now, although the domestic drama which we had

undertook to relate, has, in fact, terminated here, some of our readers may, perhaps, have felt sufficient interest in the young adventurer, of whom we have made the hero of this story, to follow him in the second part of his career; to these then, after thanking them for the kind attention they have been pleased to grant to us, we are about to recount truly and plainly, facts which a most minute research have enabled us to lay before them.

At the period we have reached, that is to say, in the month of May, 1784, the whole of Europe had fallen into that state of torpor, which unthinking men imagined to be tranquillity, but which minds more profound, regarded as the dull and momentary calm that precedes the tempest. America, by obtaining her independence, had prepared France for her revolution. Kings and people, mistrustful of each other, were upon their guard. Peter III., who had become odious to the Russians, in consequence of his ignoble character, the narrowness of his political views, and above all, for his excessive leaning to Prussian manners, and Prussian discipline, had been deposed without opposition, and strangled without a struggle. Catherine had thus found herself, at the age of thirty-two, mistress of an empire which extended over one-seventh part of the globe; her first care was to compel the neighbouring powers to accept her as a mediatrix in their quarrel, and thus become do-pendent upon her. Thus, had she obliged the people of Courland to drive from them their new Duke, Charles of Saxony, and to recall Biren; she had sent her ambassadors and her armies to Warsaw, there to have crowned by the name of Stanislaus Augustus, her former lover, Poniatowski; she had formed an alliance with England; she had associated to her policy the Courts of Vienna and Berlin; and notwithstanding all these great projects of foreign policy, she had not neglected the internal government of her own country, and in the interval of her amours, so fickle and so various, she still found time to reward industry, to encourage agriculture, to reform the laws, to raise a navy, to send Pallas into provinces the productions of which were till then unknown—Blumager into the northern Archipelago, and Bel-lings into the Indian ocean; in fine, jealous of the literary reputation of her brother, the King of Prussia, she wrote with the same hand that had ordered the erection of a new city, signed the order for the execution of young Ivan, and the dismemberment of Poland, The Refutation of the Journey into Siberia, by the Abbé Chappe, a romance of the Czarowich Chlose, several plays, among which was a translation into French of Oleg, a drama, written by the Russian poet, Dersehawin, so that Voltaire proclaimed her the Semiraris of the North, and the King of Prussia, in his letters, classed her between Solon and Lycurgus.

The effect produced amid this voluptuous and chivalric court by the arrival of such a man, as our adventurous seaman, can readily be imagined. The reputation for courage, which had rendered him the terror of the enemies of France and America, had preceded him to the court of Russia, and in exchange for his frigate, which he presented to Catherine, he received the rank of Rear-Admiral. Then the flag of Russia, after having navigated round one-half the old world, appeared in the Grecian seas, and beneath the ruins of Lacedemon and the Parthenon, he, who had assisted in establishing the independence of America, dreamt of the re-establishment of the Republics of Sparta and of Athens. The old Ottoman empire was shaken to its foundations, the defeated Turks signed a treaty of peace at Kainardji. Catherine retained Azof, Taganrog, and Kenburr, and Kenburn, compelled the Turks to grant to her the free navigation of the Black Sea, and the independence of the Crimea; she then desired to visit her new possessions. Paul, recalled to St. Petersburgh, accompanied her on this journey, the route of which had been drawn up by Potemkin. During the whole of it, all the attributes of triumph were offered to the conquering Empress and her suite; bonfires were lighted all along the road, cities were illuminated with the most fairy-like brilliancy, magnificent palaces erected, as if by magic, for one day, amid desert countries, and which the next morning disappeared; villages, rising as if beneath the wand of an enchanter, in solitudes, in which eight days before the Tartars fed their flocks; towns appearing on the horizon of which there existed but the exterior walls; in every direction, homage, and songs of welcome, and dances of the people: during the day, a numerous population crowded the road, and at night, while the Empress was sleeping, they would run to station themselves in the way she was to proceed on waking the following morning: a king and emperor rode by her side, calling themselves not her brothers, not her equals, but her courtiers; finally, a triumphal arch was erected at the last halt she was to make on her journey southward, bearing the inscription—"This is the road to Byzantium," which if it did not reveal the ambition of Catherine, demonstrated at least, the policy of Potemkin. Then Russia became strengthened in her tyranny, as America had in her independence. Catherine offered to her Admiral places which would have more than satisfied the rapacity of a courtier, honors which would have overwhelmed the ambitious, estates which would have consoled a deposed king for the loss of his dominions; but it was the deck of his ship, it was the sea with its combats and its tempests, it was the boundless immensity of ocean for which yearned the heart of our adventurous and poetic seaman. He, therefore, left the brilliant court of Catherine, as he had left the austere Congress of America, and returned to France to seek that, which he could not find elsewhere, that is to say, a life of excitement, enemies to combat, a people to defend. Paul arrived in Paris in the midst of our European wars and civil struggles; while, with one hand, we were seizing a foreign enemy by the throat, with the other, we were tearing our own entrails. That king, whom he had seen ten years before, beloved, honored, powerful, was then a captive, despised and strengthless. All that had been exalted was abased, and great names fell as did high-born heads.—It was the reign of equality, and the guillotine was the levelling instrument. Paul inquired after Emanuel, and was told that he was proscribed. He asked what had become of his mother, and was informed that she was dead. Then he felt an irresistible longing to revisit once again, before he himself might die, the spot on which, twelve years before, he had experienced emotions at once so sweet and terrible. He set out for Brittany, left his carriage at Vannes, and mounted on horseback, as he had done on the first day he had seen Marguerite; but he was no longer the young and enthusiastic seaman, whose desires and hopes had no horizon; he was a man bereft of all those, brilliant illusions, for he had tasted of all, whether weet or bitter, had learnt to appreciate all, both men and things; had known all, glory and oblivion. Therefore, did he not come to search a family, but to visit tombs.

When he came within sight of the castle, he turned his eyes toward Achard's house, and not being able to discover it, he thought he would go into the forest, but the forest seemed to have vanished as by enchantment. It had been sold as national property to twenty-five or thirty farmers of the neighbourhood, who had cleared off the timber, and transformed it into a large plain. The gigantic oak had disappeared, and the plough had passed over the unknown grave of the Count de Morlaix, and the eyes of his son even, could no longer recognize the spot.

Then he returned through the park toward the castle, now become even more gloomy and desolate than when he had last seen it. In it he found only an old man, a living ruin amidst these ruins of the past; it was at first intended to have pulled down the mansion, but the reputation for holiness which the marchioness had left behind her, was regarded with such religious veneration throughout the country, that the old walls, which for four centuries had been the abode of her ancestors, remained undesecrated. Paul went through the apartments, which for three years had remained closed, and which were now open for him. He walked through the portrait gallery; it was in the same state as he had formerly seen it; no pious hand had added to the portrait either of the marquis or the marchioness. He went into the study in which he had been concealed—found a book lying in it which he had opened and placed upon the very spot on which he found it, and read the same passages which he had read so many years before. He then pushed open the door which communicated with the contract chamber, where had passed the chief scenes of that drama in which he was the principal actor. The table was still in the same place and the Venetian looking-glass over the chimney-piece was there, shattered as it had been by the ball of Emanuels pistol.

Paul advanced to the fire-place, and placing his elbow on the marble mantle-piece, questioned the servant as to the last years of the Marchioness.

The account he received shewed that she had remained austere and melancholy, as was her wont. Remaining secluded and alone at the castle, her hours were uniformly spent in three different places: her oratory, the vault in which the body of her husband had been buried, and the spot sheltered by the oak tree, at the foot of which her lover had been interred. For eight years after the evening on which Paul had taken leave of her, she had been seen to wander amid the old corridors of the castle, and in the gloomy avenues of the Park, slow and pale as a spectre; then a disease of the heart, engendered by the agonies she had suffered, declared itself, and she daily became weaker. At length, one evening, when her failing strength no longer permitted her to walk, she had ordered the servants to carry her to the foot of the oak tree, her favorite walk, that she might once more see, she said, the sun setting in the ocean. When they had reached the spot, she desired the servants to withdraw, and to come back to her in half an hour. On their return they found her lying fainting on the ground. They immediately bore her to the castle, but having recovered her senses on the way, she ordered them, instead of conducting her to her own room, which they usually did, to take her down into the family vault. There she had still strength enough to kneel upon the tomb of her husband, and made a sign that she desired to be left alone. However imprudent their doing so might be, the servants elbow on the marble withdrew, for she had accustomed them to obey her in every thing at the first intimation of her will. They, however, remained at a short distance, concealed behind the corner of a tomb, that they might be ready to render her assistance, should it be necessary. In a few minutes they saw her fall down upon the stone on which she had been praying; they rushed forward, imagining that she had again fainted. She was dead.

Paul requested the old servant to conduct him into the vault, and slowly entered it with uncovered head; and when he had reached the stone which covered the grave of his mother, he knelt down and prayed. On the monumental stone were inscribed the following words, and which may still be seen in one of the chapels of the church of the small town of Auray, to which it has since been removed. The inscription had been written by the marchioness herself, and she had desired that it should be placed upon her tomb.

"Here lies the very noble and very puissant lady Marguerite Blanche de Sablé, Marchioness of Auray; born the 2nd of August 1729—died the 3rd September, 1788.

"Pray for her and for her children."

Paul raised his eyes to heaven, with an expression of infinite gratitude, His mother, who during her life, had for so long a time forgotten him, had remembered him in her funeral inscription.

Six months after this visit, the National Convention decreed, in solemn sitting, that they would attend in a body the funeral procession of Paul Jones, formerly a commodore in the American navy, and whose burial was to take place in the cemetery of Pere La Chaise.

They had come to this decision, said the decree, in order to consecrate the establishment of religious freedom throughout France.